Parts of a World

A. G. MOJTABAI

Parts of a World

A Novel

TRIQUARTERLY BOOKS

NORTHWESTERN UNIVERSITY PRESS

EVANSTON, ILLINOIS

Northwestern University Press
www.nupress.northwestern.edu

The epigraph (translated by A. G. Mojtabai) is from
Muertes y maravillas by Jorge Teillier, copyright 1971,
used by permission of Editorial Universitaria, Santiago,
Chile.

Printed in the United States of America

10 9 8 7 6 5 4 3 2 1

Library of Congress Cataloging-in-Publication Data
Mojtabai, A. G., 1937–
    Parts of a world : a novel / A. G. Mojtabai.
      p. cm. — (TriQuarterly fiction)
    ISBN-13: 978-0-8101-2766-1 (cloth : alk. paper)
    ISBN-10: 0-8101-2766-0 (cloth : alk. paper)
    1. Social workers—New York (State)—New
York—Fiction. 2. New York (N.Y.)—Fiction. I. Title.
PS3563.O374P37 2011
813'.54—dc22
                                   2011000508

remembering

MATT

a lamp gone out

unfading light

When everyone leaves for other planets
I will stay in the abandoned city . . .

—Jorge Teillier, "Cuando todos se vayan,"
in *Muertes y maravillas*

I believe
with perfect faith
in the coming of the Messiah.
Though he tarry,
I will wait for him . . .
I believe.

—"Ani Ma'amin," Jewish morning prayer

CONTENTS

I

II

Parts of a World

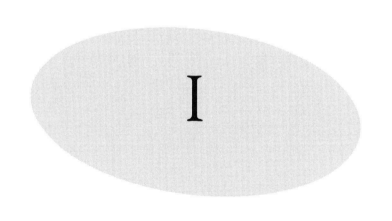

I

1

Imprimis

Forget? Tell me how.

I'm in the subway, Fifty-Ninth Street, piling into the down-town express when . . . who's that, looking just like him, starting slantwise up the steps? But I'm trapped; the doors heave to with a hard sigh; a stranger's fingers drill into my back. I spin round to reply when—stair and station hurtling past—I lose him, I'll never know.

Out of nowhere he appears—once, even on the upscale Upper East Side. Men in fine suits raced out of offices, their silk ties swing-ing. He moved slowly, a shabby, solitary figure among the suits, in the crowd but not of it. *At least he's employed,* I told myself, glimps-ing a company logo on the pocket of his shirt. Coming closer, I pieced it out: AIR IDEAL—and the face, the face! Can't imagine why I'd ever—

No, but if I found him—*knew* it was Michael? Say I stumbled across him, huddled in some deserted doorway, coiled head to knees, hands retracted, drawn up, deep in his sleeves for warmth . . . doing his best to hide, melt into shadow.

Would I be able to walk on by?

My name is Tom—Tom Limbeck. Social worker for more than

two decades. Still at it, and still something of a misfit in my profession. I'm told I think too much, it's hard to be natural. I used to make home visits; but no more: I'm mostly a paper pusher these days. It was Michael's case that drew me down into the streets again.

I don't know who dubbed him "Saint Francis of the Dumpsters." Misplaced in obvious ways—he had no followers, he never shared his dream—the label stuck, nonetheless; it wasn't entirely inapt. His refusal to strike back when attacked, or even to admit injury, might have passed for peacefulness if you weren't familiar with his history. His poverty? More inevitable than chosen, I think. But he held fast, he refused to relinquish his dream. Perhaps it was that mind-squint, his monomaniacal burning focus (shared by saints and paranoiacs alike) which prompted the comparison.

Absolutism, in his case, conjoined with such mildness—I could not grasp it.

I could not *fathom* it—hampered as I was by my own squint, a family disability, lovingly cultivated, long in the making. It's hard to explain even to myself . . .

My father was a devout atheist—I have to begin with that. Nothing so energized and delighted him as the skewering of belief. I learned to breathe within his strictures, to "suppose that" or "for the sake of argument assume," but as a result, to this day, I cannot say I believe—anything. Always, always, I hedge my bets. I shift from foot to foot.

Both my parents were lapsed Catholics. "Inactive" they call such now. Gentler times, I'm tempted to say, but what do I know? We kept in contact with grandparents and aunts and uncles who persisted in the faith and, to their credit, never disowned or shunned us, although I'm sure that many Masses and petitions were offered up in our behalf. When the priest paid a visit to my grandmother in the hospital, I excused myself but waited right outside the door, impatient for him to do whatever he'd come to do, then leave. I can still hear it . . . the scratch of dry bread breaking. A litany:

"Here is true sorrow.
Here is perfect sorrow. Blessed are we
who are called to this sorrow . . ."

The words were so outlandish that I let out a laugh. I doubt if anyone heard me, but cleared my throat and coughed to cover the sound, just in case.

My father insisted that I'd misheard, mixed up a couple of words, yet conceded that I'd caught the *drift* of them accurately enough. I do know that my grandmother prayed for "a happy death"—those were her words exactly, and she repeated them as the time grew near. It was plain that she thought me a callow youth, for her last words to me (spoken well before the end while she was still in her right mind) were to wish that I be granted "the gift of tears." Some happy! Some gift! Her language was more than foreign, it was downright spooky to me. I never thought of faith as sugary or safe, as most people seemed to—quite the contrary.

We—my sister and I—grew up without. My father was a chemist and his favorite reply to any and all believers was the one that Galileo, facing the Inquisition, whispered to himself, "Nevertheless, the earth does move . . ."

"Sit stand sit stand! It's how they keep you from falling asleep." My father's litany of insults to adult intelligence perpetrated by the Church did not end there. There were throat blessings with forked candles, foreheads smudged with ash, self-blinding: dimmed lights, eyes blurred by the fog of incense and the desire not to see clearly. What irked him most was what he called "the mental crouch," summed up by all the kneeling. "Only thing I'd go down on my knees for is a heart attack," he boasted more than once and, by curious coincidence, that's how it happened for him. Poetic justice, some would say. He was shutting off a valve under the sink, trying to stem a water leak; it was a valve in his heart that gave way. The water seeped and seeped . . .

Anyhow.

That's how it was. What I can say is that my family wanted

nothing to do with faith and managed without it. And how can you miss what you've never known? Looking back, though, on the subject of death for instance, I think it's fair to say that we were more than a little uneasy. None of the usual evasions were available to us. While we prided ourselves on our "reason" and "realism," refusing to airbrush any unpleasant facts or to fall for any version, literal or metaphoric, of the fantasy of resurrection, we practiced our own form of make-believe and were skilled evaders in our own fashion. My father was cremated without ceremony; he was "missed" rather than mourned. There'd been Eddie, my older brother, a door forever shut. Then—a younger brother, born prematurely, whose name I never knew. Born and gone. I remember asking repeatedly "Where do *people* go?" (I knew where animals went), and the question being ignored each time as if I'd never spoken.

When did the unspoken become sealed off—become unspeakable?

I'm not straying, but struggling, here . . .

What I'm trying to get a handle on is the tangle of motive. Why, aside from my legitimate concern for his health and safety, his very survival, was I so haunted by Michael's case, that one case among so many others? Why did I persist, relentlessly chipping away at his secret (his faith/his delusion), why did I became so consumed by the need to find him out, to see for myself what he saw? Was it only to refute him, the better to confront him with the real world? To *invite* him into the real world would have been the gentler, wiser course, but I hadn't the luxury of time. And, hardest of all to admit, I hadn't, finally, the patience. I pushed and wouldn't let up, as if my own sanity—my salvation, if you will—were at stake in keeping the boundaries clear. I see that now, I didn't then.

If only I could be done with him, once and for all!

2

Presenting

I'm trying to recapture our first meeting . . . I recall giving myself a full hour to go over his file beforehand, but this was my custom, nothing out of the usual.

Nor did his case seem to be anything out of the usual at first. Hard luck, plain and simple. Still . . . I pored over the drawing Michael had made during his last hospitalization to see if I could find a hidden figure, a trace, or some sort of encrypted message—a knot to chew on. Why take the trouble to preserve such a scrap otherwise?

It was a pencil sketch of an outdoor scene, house and trees without shading, the sky a mere stripe confined to the upper frame—a lid. Preschoolers picture sky like this.

At the dead center of the page he'd placed a house: windowless, square, flat-roofed, nothing but a box, a sarcophagus, almost. (*Or a Dumpster . . . ?* Hard to banish the thought.) A path arrowed straight to the middle of the box, aimed at what should have been a door, but there was no door. He hadn't forgotten the chimney on what passed for a roof, complete with its scribble of smoke. The heads of the flowers and of the trees bordering the path and the clouds overhead (detached from the sky) were drawn with the same scribble. Not much weight to any of it, no real difference between one thing and another—a puff, and all away.

In front of the house stood this tiny stick figure (whether male or female, no way to tell), its arms bare sticks. He'd left off hands, the scallops or twig clusters that even very young children insist upon for hands. There was one other thing, next to the stick figure: a birdhouse on a pole, complete in loving detail, with pitched roof, arched doorway, a porthole for a window with three little dot-heads peeping out, and a tiny chimney with its own little corkscrew of smoke. To the birds he'd given a complete, a real, home.

Holding the picture up to the light, I noticed—or *thought* I noticed—a thinning of the paper, sign of a strong erasure next to the stick person. But I couldn't be sure. Turning the page over, I saw that someone had printed the date and some words on the other side—had found it important enough to pass this on as case material. A few words trying to make sense of it: "His home? Early memory? His *IDEA* of home?"

Anyone reading, or even simply skimming, Michael's file would recognize this scene as sheer fantasy, the dream of a memory—the memory of that dream, twice removed from reality. I was curious to know what Michael's earliest memories actually were but refrained from asking anything but the standard. At least the circumstances of his birth were a matter of record. He'd been found, thickly wrapped in newspaper, in a Dumpster near the George Washington Bridge. An NYPD officer on foot patrol thought he heard kittens and lifted the lid to check. Not a unique situation, I'm afraid, and not the worst case—far from it. There's a whole section of a cemetery upstate devoted to cases of this kind, as I discovered recently. The infants are all named Hope—Amanda Hope, Johnny Hope, and so on. Lot of little hopes buried in that ground . . . But now I *am* straying . . .

As it turned out, Michael was spared the worst. Born prematurely, weighing less than four pounds, he'd been rushed over to prenatal intensive care at Columbia Presbyterian and somehow managed to survive the day. I assumed that the true story of his birth—the Dumpster detail at least—was unknown to Michael.

Who would be so cruel as to tell him? His mother had been located months after the drop-off. She'd wandered back to the site in a daze and had been carted off to the hospital (a separate hospital, mental). Michael had long since become a ward of the state. The mother, fourteen at the time, had never known she was pregnant. Beyond a list of her hospitalizations over the years following that birth, Michael's file contained no further information concerning her. Whether the records trailed off or (all too likely) had been mislaid, no one had tried to follow up. Of his father: nothing at all on file.

The referral was from the outpatient department of B—— after one of Michael's increasingly frequent hospitalizations. He was still considered severely depressed but, thanks to the latest psychotropics, able to live and work on the outside. Dr. Kirsch would continue as med manager, monitoring Michael's prescriptions. All told, the list of medications he'd tried made quite a litany: Thorazine, Ativan, Navane, Haldol, Prolixin. Zyprexa, Zoloft (who names these things?), Klonopin, Risperdal . . . There was no guarantee that he'd continue taking his medications on schedule. That's where I came in. I was to arrange for a halfway house, provide regular supervision, and facilitate job interviews.

He was twenty-eight—older than he looked—and, considering how he'd been living, not too punishingly underweight. Semi-educated: he'd made it through the second year of high school. Four foster home placements, none permanent, thanks to his habit of running away. His employment record was spotty and, predictably, noncompetitive—busboy, janitorial aide, stock boy in a warehouse, thrift shop sales assistant. A couple of sheltered workshops in between. What he liked best, he'd told one of his employers, was doing the same thing over and over. Maybe he wanted to count on things holding steady from day to day—a kind of safety in that—or maybe it was simply the numbing brought on by repetitive motion that he found soothing.

In his spare time, he collected cans, bottles, glossy magazines, whatever he could trade on the street. Some items he kept for himself. In this way, I was to learn later, he'd managed to accumulate a small library of tattered paperbacks and had become something of a reader.

He'd been living—subsisting would be more accurate—in abandoned apartment houses, condemned as fire traps and unfit for human habitation, bare shells of buildings with no running water, the staircases broken off between floors. He'd camped for months on a warehouse lot, bedding down in a refrigerator box, folding it up and hiding it by day, until it got lost or lifted. He'd been picked up in bus stations and subway tunnels, and had been caught napping on empty late-night subway cars shuttling back and forth from Bronx to the Battery, where even on the best nights homeless riders manage only a few hours of unbroken sleep. From late April to mid-November, he often found accommodation out on the street, on a park bench or in the entryway to a shop, consenting to sleep in shelters only in emergencies, transported there under coercion, when rounded up by the police.

On the whole, his file wasn't all that helpful, though. I could see why. My own first impression is barely recoverable from my official notes, muffled as they are by the peculiar jargon of my trade:

> Client initiated no discussion. Upon questioning, answered in some detail, but often with flat, or inappropriate, affect. Avoided eye contact. Extreme nervousness when spoken to at close range. Denied ever hearing voices.

That business of "flat affect"—it was a formula. I might as well have written "an appearance (calculated?) of imperturbable calm," or "a keeper-of-secrets deadpan." He could have been merely bored. After all, he'd been through this ritual before.

What little he did speak was hard to follow—monotone, for the most part, though the volume or pitch of a particular word was liable to shift suddenly, giving an extra weight, or a sort of halo to it, some special significance I failed to grasp. The toilet flushing next door did nothing to help matters, nor did the fact that my radiator was acting up, creating a chatter of its own, a chiding, chuckling sound.

He complained about the last hospital he'd been in—all the tests.

"Tests?" I examined the record more carefully. According to the official reports, he'd performed well enough on the neuropsychologicals: the VSAT, Picture Completion, Trails, and Fingertapping, also on Verbal Fluency and Proverbs.

"Yes . . . what about the tests? You were starting to say—?"

"Oh, you know: Is blue up or down? Tell us the difference between singing and sighing. Sad is to sick as sorry is to what? Questions like that."

When I asked about his treatment, his voice became high-pitched in mimicry of one of the nurses: "Leave everything to us. Let us worry about that. All you have to do is take the pills."

He named his medications—with astonishing accuracy.

"Guess they never hit on the magic mixture," I said to be saying something.

The medicines were bad enough, he said, but the worst thing was electroshock, trying to jolt him out of his memories.

"Bad memories?" I ventured.

"I forget." (His idea of a joke?) But I knew I'd been pressing my luck.

One thing he was willing to recall: A couple of times, they'd put him in a room where, he claimed, the walls were Teflon. They called it "the quiet room," because in it you could scream as much and as loud as you wanted and nobody heard or cared.

I busied myself with the intake questionnaire. Grateful for the ritual, actually—I needed a minute to recoup, to strategize. I knew what sort of assistance was needed but had to think how best to say why he'd been on the street and why he needed some sort of protected living arrangement. I walked my pen down the page slowly, carefully. I considered the line "Harm to Self." That would have landed him back in a psychiatric ward, so I kept on going down the list. Michael wasn't on the streets because of rent increase, expired lease or eviction, travel mishap, job relocation, alcohol or drug abuse. Only the "ISO" (In Search Of) category seemed apropos: "To Get Food." Even then, I suspected that food wasn't the main thing, merely a cover for it. My pen stumbled over another item on the list: "Faith-related." I paused. Stared at it. Was this something new? Funny, how I'd never noticed it before. I couldn't think of a single case that applied.

What else can I say about Michael, my first impression?

He wasn't at all impressive. Passing him on the street, you wouldn't look twice. Light brown hair, middling height, medium build, a slouch. Up close, only one feature stood out: his eyes, so widely spaced they gave him a look of perpetual wonderment, and their peculiar shade, whether pale blue or gray, or changing with the light, I never got close enough to tell. He wore chinos, scuffed desert boots. Two sweatshirts. The outer one with the hood, which I persuaded him to peel off so as not to get overheated, was unmarked; the one under that had a Sooners logo. It looked very old and one elbow was torn. I asked him if he'd ever actually been to Oklahoma. He nodded. "Pretty much everywhere," he said. His record—the long list of "incidents" and arrests in bus stations across the country—bore him out.

I was struck by how slope-shouldered he seemed—stooped, as though someone were leaning, pressing against him, pushing him forward, despite the counter-pull of his backpack. His backpack: an item which I was only once to see him without. An item with more of a story attached, I might add, and one more thing I'll come to in its own time.

"Why do you think you're here?" I ventured.

He shrugged. Our faces were turned to one another, but his eyes did not meet mine. I asked him the reason for his last hospitalization. "Reason . . ." he repeated as though the word were new to him.

"How come?" I prompted. When I jogged his memory, he acknowledged that some man—a street person, a stranger—had "come on" to him but not that he'd been raped and beaten unconscious. Not that he'd been left for dead with a concussion so severe the emergency room physician didn't think he'd make it. "You might not have survived, you realize that?"

Again he shrugged.

"You might've died! Don't you have any *feeling* about it?"—more a shout than a question.

But the feeling was all on my side, apparently. My outburst met with thick silence, an empty stare. I was reminded of one of those wall charts that keeps popping up on psych wards: "Words for Feelings"—"mad . . . sad . . . bad . . . glad . . ." how important it was for a patient like Michael to name what he was feeling—to *own* that feeling.

"And I see you've been hospitalized for dysentery in the past . . ." The conclusion was inescapable: "We've got to get you off the street."

As I phoned, casting about for the best placement, I watched him rummage around in his backpack. It was stuffed—"everything but the kitchen sink," I was tempted to say—but then I spotted actual pipe fittings in the mix. I guess he hoped to sell them. I spied, too, a kid's notebook with a speckled cover, a tangle of socks, a mess of fast food freebies—napkins, plastic cutlery, and a handful of ketchup packets.

He gathered up his things, shouldered his backpack, and stood patiently by while I wrote out directions to St. Joseph's hostel, the halfway house uptown, and doled out subway tokens. He lingered after I'd finished, seemingly at a loss as to what the signals for closure or dismissal might be, so I rose from my desk, led the way to the door, and opened it.

We paused again in the hallway. I'd be checking that he arrived safely, I warned. "I don't want you taking any detours." I repeated the time of our follow-up meeting: I'd written it all out. I reminded him that he'd just stuffed my note into his backpack, not to forget.

He turned halfway down the hall, an afterthought, and then— did I imagine this?—nodded, folded one knee in the faintest of bows, the ghost of a genuflection.

I'm sure of what I heard, though, his parting shot:

"Mercy bucket!"

"What?" Oh . . . "*Merci beaucoup*! I get it. You've studied a little French . . ." and I laughed, as I figured I was supposed to do.

3

Gestures

Michael kept all his appointments with me for the first few weeks and he was consistently on time. No breakthroughs, of course—none expected. We were simply coasting (at best), but that seemed movement enough for a start. I needed to create trust and knew this would take a while. For the time being, I contented myself with establishing our routine.

Once he'd settled himself, backpack carefully positioned between his feet or nestled in his lap, I'd break the silence that was sure to follow by asking, "How are you?" or "What's new?" He'd shrug to either question, but I'd start out the same way, regardless, each and every time.

To "where are you now?" his eyes would shift from corner to corner, seeking a literal place, fixing at last on some vanishing point beyond the wall. He never leaned back, never removed his jacket, and always seemed ready to bolt. My "getting kind of hot in here, isn't it?" prompted no reply—the jacket stayed on.

When he seemed off in a world of his own, I'd try to summon him back by asking, "Where are we now?"—giving him cause to throw the presumptive "we" back in my face, but he let the provocation pass. He let all provocations pass. I know that he heard me because, more than once, I caught him whispering back, whether to himself or by way of answer to me, I couldn't tell:

"I know where I am."

I should explain that while I'm not really a psychotherapist, I often think of myself as a poor man's version of one—a bureaucratic ear for hire. I don't keep a box of tissues on top of my desk, though I do have a supply close to hand, tucked away in my second drawer. Clients rarely weep in my presence; they're more apt to rant and rave.

It's painful to realize that this account turns out to be more about me than Michael. Yet how could it be otherwise? When Michael shut me out, what was I left with? Add to this my resolve not to rush things or to trespass, well aware that if I did, he'd simply raise the ramparts round himself, fortifying his isolation. A slow breaching of the walls already in place was my plan, a search for structural faults. I vowed to be patient—to be Patience itself—and wait for an opening. I can't say I always held back, even in my best-behavior days at the beginning. The few times I gave in to this or that pressure of circumstance and pushed, the push-back from Michael was swift. I'd understood all along that it would get me nowhere.

But—coming back to the little I was permitted to know . . . He'd settled in at St. Joe's, the halfway house to which I'd directed him. He tended to miss meals, yet returned faithfully to shower and sleep. As time wore on, he found a temporary job off the books as a dishwasher; according to Father Evans, reports were that he was getting along at work as well. And he was taking his medications as prescribed. By his own admission, he still spent most of his free time on the street, making his rounds of the Dumpsters; he claimed the reason was economic: "collecting" was how he kept up his income. Except for his absence at mealtimes, there was only one other problem. St. Joe's refused to accommodate some of his Dumpster finds, objecting to the roaches and to the stench that accompanied them. But Michael dealt with this situation as a responsible adult, renting a locker at a warehouse in the Bronx; he was able to afford the luxury now.

My caseload was heavy enough without Michael, so I was pleased to stretch out the intervals—three weeks, a month—between appointments.

It was summer when things changed.

The police picked him up in Brooklyn. He'd been loitering. Scared the daylights out of some kids playing in Prospect Park and made their parents frantic.

He'd crashed the birthday party of a five-year-old and had been caught in the act, laughing and singing and jerking the guy ropes on the "bouncy house" (one of those air-pumped play houses made of industrial-strength plastic) designed for kids to jump around inside. The children had been having a wonderful time until Michael decided to add to the fun by tugging on the ropes, giving the bouncy house a few extra shakes, extra thrills for the little ones, and one of the older girls started screaming. He still couldn't understand why the police had been summoned, why all the fuss.

"You simply can't do that," I tried.

"Do what?"

"Hang around like you did. You've got to let the little kids alone."

"Not to sing?" He seemed genuinely upset now: "appropriate affect" in this instance. "I didn't mean—"

"It's not what you meant. It's what people *think* you meant." And I tried my best to explain why the parents' concerns were justified, even though I could tell I wasn't making much of an impression.

"Do you understand? The reason for people being upset?"

Perhaps he nodded. Perhaps faintly. Signifying assent? Perhaps. One could only hope so. He'd avoid bouncy houses in the future; that was the most anyone could count on. As Michael saw it, he'd simply been playing. He'd been filled with happiness at the children's happiness, and then—all in the spirit of spreading joy—with the thrill of scaring them.

According to the police report, Michael never stopped smiling, smiling and gesturing and singing out as he tugged on those ropes—it looked like enticement. And he'd kept on smiling all the way to the station.

The rest of our session accomplished nothing. I'd heard that he wasn't showing up regularly for meals at the hostel and only picking at his plate when he did show. I asked him why. It might not be gourmet food, but it was sure to be nutritious and clean, and he'd save money.

"Know how you spell 'hostel'?" he asked. Then he answered his own question: "h-o-s-t-i-l-e!"

"Why do you say that? Isn't the place friendly?"

But all I got by way of reply was the depthless stare, the ghostly smile.

Once again I warned him about Dumpster-diving, or "Dumpster-dining," as he preferred to call it—a distinction without a difference in my book.

Even then I knew how useless—how unpersuaded he'd be. There was no way anyone could keep track of him twenty-four hours a day unless I had him recommitted.

When he stood up to leave, he asked something about the door.

"What's that?" I was already busy jotting down notes.

"The door—should I shut it?"

"Yes, yes, of course," I said. He knew the routine. He'd never asked before.

Always, an after-burn . . . With Michael there were no casual remarks; he spoke so seldom. Around the least thing he said, there seemed to lurk a large intention. Only when the door closed did I reflect his question back upon myself. *"Not to sing?"* . . . Was *this* what I was asking of Michael—that he shut the door on childhood, never to join the celebration?

4

Incidents

I could hear Gary shouting.

Both clients showed up early for their appointments that Monday afternoon. My doors were shut so I had no idea what was going on in the anteroom. I glanced at my appointment schedule: Michael at one thirty, Gary at two; if Gary happened to arrive early, that was his business.

I opened my door to find Gary looming over Michael, shaking a chocolate bar in his face. He must have tried to ram it down Michael's throat. And Michael must have resisted: his lips were white with clenching; there was a muddy swipe across his cheek from lip to ear. Gary was shouting, "Dumbass! Can't talk? Can't open your mouth?" Shrinking into his chair, with bent head, eyes cast down (an eyelid twitching), Michael was a textbook-perfect picture of submission. When Gary turned to greet me with "I got here first," and I answered in no uncertain terms: "Michael was scheduled before you," I could just barely make out Michael's voice in the background, his faint (meant to be disarming?) "*Was* I?"

"That's enough!"—I stepped in between the two—"You're up first, Michael. We go according to schedule here." And, hand on Michael's shoulder, I gently nudged him forward into the sanctuary of my office. Even with the door shut, Gary's taunts trailed after us. His "Be my guest!" and "Good riddance!" were impossible to miss.

Knowing Gary's temper, I fully expected that he'd storm out. He surprised me, though, by waiting. He needn't have bothered. Sullen, simmering with resentment, he spent most of his appointment time tapping his feet and staring at the backs of his hands. I can't say that Michael's session went all that much better. When I tried to make him understand that he had certain rights, that he shouldn't let people push him around, all he had to say was, "It's nothing, really."

"Nothing? In what way nothing? Nothing—meaning *you don't care*? Or nothing of importance?" I gave him a minute or two to sort it out, then, unable to wait, blustered, "I can't hear you!"

But Michael wasn't saying, there was nothing to hear. So I answered for him. Far from nothing, there was a vital principle at stake here, a matter of self-respect, of standing up for himself. And there was the question of survival. I couldn't imagine how Michael managed to keep himself alive out on the streets for as long as he had.

Meanwhile, Gary was pacing right outside the door. Then he started laughing, great gulps of laughter. There was no way Michael could have failed to notice this—at the very least, a powerful distraction—but Michael gave no sign of hearing anything unusual. My session with him never came into focus.

Both their sessions turned out to be a waste of time, Michael and Gary refusing even to mention what had happened between them. I counted myself lucky to have witnessed the two of them together with my own eyes and had drawn at least one appropriate cautionary conclusion: the need to rearrange Gary's next appointments so as to never—if I could help it—permit his path and Michael's to cross again.

And that was merely a starter to my week . . . Next morning, Karina called us into emergency session. She'd found a suicide note dropped in the suggestion box. The box was kept at the front intake desk, available to everyone. Most of the time, all it held was a clutter of complaints from the staff: stale coffee, pilfered snacks, too much noise, too heavy caseload expectations. Once in a while, something mischievous turned up, like "Think outside the box!" We opened the box once a week—*if* anyone happened to remember. So imagine our consternation at finding a predeath announcement for "next Thursday." Since there was no date and we'd been remiss, "next Thursday" might have meant *this* Thursday. The note was unsigned, no remedy proposed. And no one present could think of a client who might have written such a note. Someone's idea of a joke? A very sick joke?

We passed the note around. The handwriting was foreign; the shape of the letters reminded me of what little I knew of Greek, the "d" a "delta" with its scorpion tail, the "e" a delicate side-tipped trident, an "epsilon." One of *my* clients? I couldn't think of one but decided it best to double-check my files as soon as a free moment presented itself.

Although attendance wasn't taken, whenever I noticed eyes circling, I knew that others were making a silent tally, asking, *Anybody missing?* I wasn't the only one spooked.

"Don't try and talk me out of this" was how the message began.

I made it through my morning schedule, jittery all the while. It wasn't until lunchtime that I found a moment to check my files. I found no Greeks, no writing samples remotely resembling the handwriting in the suicide note, and I couldn't picture a client of mine concocting anything like it.

By the time I'd gone through the files, my lunch hour was two-thirds gone, and it was only then I remembered that I'd agreed to take June out for a birthday lunch. Too late to do anything but beg off, I phoned the restaurant and left a message that I'd been unavoidably detained at the office. I didn't find out until later, but by the time I called, my guilt was already compounded—June's purse had been stolen.

Having lived with her for some years now, I thought I knew a few things about June, but her surprise—the culprit had been white, not black, not even Latino—took me by surprise. Why shouldn't he be white?

What's more, he'd been so very polite. When he stooped over

to pick up the napkin she'd dropped, she'd been moved to compliment him on his thoughtfulness.

What color hair? The police needed to know. She wasn't sure. Dark blond or light brown, an in-between shade, nothing unusual. Had she been able to take a good look at his face? Eyes blue or brown? She couldn't say. Hazel, possibly? Possibly . . . Nothing, it seemed, had impressed June so much as the man's correctness, his whiteness.

If I hadn't been held up at the office (she was convinced), none of this would have happened.

The puzzling part was how unlikely that anyone in need, and desperate enough to do this, would be found dining at Marty's. The menu, posted on the window and outside door, would have been a strong deterrent. But this young man appeared prosperous enough. Dressed as he was in a nubby, earth-toned tweed jacket with a brown turtleneck, he might have passed for a bond trader or a corporate lawyer. Then again, thinking it over, June wondered, "Loafers with tassels . . . tassels and tweed?" Something a little fishy there?

But, all told, a well-groomed, nice young man. And, as she said, *white*.

He'd taken his time, too. After paying his bill, he'd paused long enough to double-count his tip. She remembered that part distinctly. Had he even smiled in her direction? June wouldn't have put it past him. The coolness of his performance, his unshakable poise, stunned her. She thought he'd been carrying a briefcase when he got up to leave, but maybe it was actually her handbag; he was brazen enough to carry it off in plain sight. The nerve of him—the *chutzpah!*—she couldn't get over it.

Because she'd been expecting me, June had settled at one of the larger tables. Had I been there, she wouldn't have spread out, slinging her handbag by its strap over the back of the empty chair by way of advertising the fact that she was reserving a place for someone coming to join her at any moment—that she wasn't alone. This arrangement left her handbag exposed for easy lifting, particularly with her head turned to the door, as it often was, because—*same theme*—she expected to see me coming through that door each time it opened. Cause and effect; the sequence was iron-clad. If I'd shown up on time as promised, she wouldn't have done these things; none of it would have happened.

The waiter had set down her bowl of carrot-fennel soup with a hearty "Enjoy!" Sentence fragments—like "Have a happy!" or "Have a good one!"—always irked her. Good one *what*? But an objectless "enjoy!" turned out to be the least of her irritations, for it was at exactly that moment that she first noticed her handbag was missing.

As the waiters turned the place upside down in search of the handbag, June's soup went cold. She'd refused all their efforts at consolation—the main course special and dessert free of charge, the soup reheated or a fresh bowlful.

The police officer taking notes warned June about the very real danger of identity theft, advising her to cancel her credit cards immediately. "And better change all your locks if you want to sleep in your apartment tonight," he'd added.

I came home to find June in a state. She'd eaten nothing since breakfast so was bound to be cranky. I was not in the finest of moods myself. Knowing nothing about the events of June's day, my first shock on returning was to find my keys suddenly useless. I could hear June's voice on the telephone, so I knew she was inside, but couldn't imagine why she was locking me out. I pounded and shouted, until I heard the eye-slot lifting and her voice: "That you?"

"Who else! Who else would it be!"

At the end of a very brief police interview, June asked what the chances of nabbing the thief might be. "Virtually nil," the officer assured her. "How about simply getting back my bag?" she persisted. "It was a good one—a Gucci."

"Don't expect anything," he advised.

"When did I ever?" June gave a little laugh, recounting this, and stared pointedly at me.

I proposed dining out on the weekend by way of reparation, but June was unbending. "Don't bother," she said. "I've lost my appetite." And—as for Marty's—she'd vowed never to set foot in the place again.

5

Trying: A Social Occasion

"Is that the shower I hear dripping again?" June asked. "Could you not let it drip for once? It's really not that complicated. Just make sure it's completely turned off *before* you leave the bathroom . . ."

I was in deep shit for sure, and deeper still as I made the mistake of speaking my resolution aloud: "I'll try and have a good time."

"If you have to try, forget it," June snapped back. "I don't understand you!" She gave a loud sigh. Her eyebrows, steeply angled, higher than true, signaled astonishment or alarm; she'd overdone the tweezing and I had the feeling she blamed me for that, too.

Now, standing in front of the bedroom mirror, she kept turning her head from side to side trying to make up her mind which earring to wear, a long, silvery dangle in one ear, a golden hoop in the other.

"The Western ear is best," I advised.

"The *what?*" she said, her voice rising.

"Starboard ear, I think."

"Let's not say another word until it starts," she proposed, setting both earrings aside and reinserting the small gold studs she wore every day; they looked like nail heads to me, although I'd never say so. It would just set her off. I don't know why women have this urge to mutilate themselves. "I hope you'll at least be civil when they come," she added, breaking her own rule.

"Put on my party face, my party smile . . ."

"I don't know why I bother. I don't want your help."

"Tell me what you want me to do."

I had no desire to socialize, to aggregate; I refused to give way to the centripetal impulse. Only at my lowest moments in the past had I let myself be drawn into the mash. Lately, the thought occurred to me that maybe I was meant to live alone, it was as simple as that. June and I had been together for nearly four years, a record for me. My marriage—what?—eleven years ago?—had lasted barely a year. In between, I'd been "involved" with a number of women, and shacked up for a few months here and there. None of it worked out.

June was having a party for some of her office-mates at eight thirty. Said she "owed"—whatever that meant. Needless to say, I wasn't looking forward to their coming. How could I? It was my apartment, after all. *Mine*. Even so, I was making an effort—helping to get things set up, vacuuming and dusting, leaving only the mopping and waxing to June. We rarely cleaned unless about to be visited. The crud!—you couldn't imagine. So I churned up a lot of dust—with no benefit to my allergies.

Although June herself was starting to deviate, she'd laid out a small spread for the macrobiotic faithful: a sesame-miso dip along with a platter of carrots and white radish, sliced razor thin, and a huge mess of what I called "dingleberry salad"—seaweed, dulse, watercress, and whatnot. Tiny bowls of sunflower seeds and soy nuts were scattered about. I kept the kettle full and boiling for tea and did the shopping for the nonobservant—quiche, brie, water biscuits, wine, and liquor—the usual party fare. I set round candles in tea glasses and as the hour approached walked from one to the next lighting them.

Though I didn't think more ought to be required of me, I promised, for a second time, to behave, to do what I could to help out, and, once the guests arrived, put forth my best effort, trekking to

28

and fro between kitchen and living room, playing busboy, refilling glasses, gathering clutter. *In it but not of it . . .*

There were twenty-three guests jostling for standing room in my cramped living room. It was stifling—scarcely enough air to go around. Access to the bathroom was through the bedroom, so the kitchen was my only sanctuary. From there, perched on a counter stool, I listened in.

If I'd had a sip of something, things might have gone better, but I didn't feel like drinking—I rarely do—another item on June's long list of my antisocial tendencies. ("If you're not going to go macrobiotic, have a beer at least, like a regular human being," her advice on that.)

It was your standard party scene: strained laughter, a world of faking. Dim and smoky (although no one was actually smoking), the stoppered air and warm fug of too many bodies too closely packed—*where's the comfort?* People kept positioning and repositioning themselves, gassing away. "Not just rich—I mean *stinking* rich! *Gobs* of money. I'm dying to know . . ." I could make out June's voice, her party voice, shriller than everyday. "Bangalore," she said, "we're outsourcing everything including our government." Someone asked, "What?" and another answered, "Is *what* what?" Then a burst of static—laughter—obscuring speech.

"Repented?"

"Re*paint*ed!—are you kidding?" More crackling all around—a wonder things didn't combust. When the laughter flickered out, there was a serious pause. Until I heard a man say, "You've fixed up the place quite a bit. Looks good."

"Oh, I didn't do much . . ." June demurred. I silently applauded her for that. She spoiled it by going on, though: "Couple of hanging plants, I guess. My old Navajo rug—it always belonged on a wall. The poster and that pole lamp in the corner are new. From IKEA, nothing fancy . . ."

So! He'd been here before . . . News to me. It was my apartment they were talking about, the furnishings mine. June had made a few minor alterations, but it was still my pad. And June failed to mention how she'd gotten me to pull up the carpeting to buff the hardwood floor underneath. On my knees—a not-so-incidental de-tail—she forgot to mention that.

More party noises. I heard "Giuliani" quite distinctly, then "Bangalore" again and "once in a blue million," but I failed to catch the words in between. "Blm blm blem" was what it sounded like, with someone crunching ice in reply. Yet when June spoke up next, about a suicide note in a suggestion box, not one syllable was lost on me. Her complaint about my never leaving the office, even at home, was familiar enough. Then she mentioned one case squeezing out the rest—

And something about a "savior complex"—she had to be stopped!

As I traipsed out of the kitchen, I kept my sights fixed on June standing there at the center of things, chattering brightly and smil-ing to her gums. I've always found that smile of hers endearing but never have been comfortable sharing it with others—it's too naked. Anyway, she clammed up at once as I burst into their circle announcing, "Tapas, anyone?" much too loudly. (*Inappropriate af-fect,* I know.) We stood there, all three of us, temporarily deprived of speech. June glared at me. I noticed one of the men squinting into his empty glass, trying to pluck out a lone ice chip with his fingers.

"Replenish?" I asked.

"*What?*" He startled. Heads turned. One or another of us must have been loud.

"Another?" I asked, minding my decibels.

"Oh yeah, sure, I guess. Since you insist." He held out his glass.

"Here, let me." June dove in between us. Our hands collided reaching for the same prize.

We marched back to the kitchen single file, June leading, hold-ing the man's glass head-high and waving it: a piece of evidence. As soon as we crossed the threshold, she kicked the door shut. *Just us.* I was in for it. When she pitched the glass (perfectly intact) into the trash, I knew she was nearly beside herself.

"What was it you said to Malcolm?" June demanded. "Something dirty?"

"I asked him if he wanted a refill."

"How sweet of you. But that couldn't be it. It was one word, what you said. And he looked shocked."

"What word? You mean *replenish*? *That* dirty? A little moister than most, maybe . . ."

"That's dorky, Tom! Nobody ever says *replenish*. Nobody! And—by the way—refill with what?"

"Something cloudy," I improvised. "Gin and tonic, I think."

But June didn't miss a beat: "Well," she said, "I sure don't know what Malcolm was drinking and I bet you don't either. I bet you never bothered to ask—"

"What do you want me to do?"

"Act normal! Be sociable." She gave a deep sigh. "Fake it if you can't feel it. Will you do that for me, Tom, this once?"

"I don't know anybody here."

"Whose fault is that? It's pathetic! You can't keep on avoiding people—"

"I deal with people every working day of my life."

"I mean normal, successful people—not screw-ups! Happy people! You don't know any happy people—" June's eyes narrowed. "And *dealing* with people," she jabbed the air for emphasis, "isn't mingling with them. What are you *doing*?"

I'd started to struggle with the latch of the security gate covering the kitchen window; it seemed to have rusted in place. "Bad air—can't breathe. My asthma . . ."

"Allergy maybe, not asthma. Don't be so operatic!"

"You mean melodramatic."

"You *know* what I mean. What do you want, Tom? Anything?"

"Air! Need air—"

"Don't *do* this . . ." she emitted in a loud whisper. Then, full voice: "I don't have time for this . . . Fine, so run—go on! Go get a life, Tom. I've had it—"

When the latch on the security gate finally gave way, I was able

31

to pry open the window onto the fire escape. *I had to go.* No way June could miss hearing. After the groaning of the gate, a sound like the rattling of chains, iron rungs clanging as I laddered down. Hitting the ground, I toppled, kissed stone; heels of my palms—my heels—the world turned over, lampposts plunged, trees poured into the deep—

Palms scraped raw, knees grazed, the world still spinning—righted again, all wrong. Shaking . . . shaking like a leaf. Above my head, a window slammed. Above the window—spatters, stars trembled. Connect the dots, the blinking dots . . . I could not.

Seconds?—minutes?—passed.

Once I regained my breath, once everything stilled, became solid, rooted again, my relief was palpable. I felt better now, much better: solid, decisive, and—no other word for it—*replenished.*

6

Missing

Michael's next appointment was a no-show. Still, I kept his slot open and my door ajar. I could have moved up my other appointments, freeing me to leave the office before five, but chose (once again) to stick with the schedule as written. The two clients who'd arrived early seemed to be in no hurry, so I waited out Michael's empty time on the chance that he might show up late with some sort of excuse.

Mrs. R, the next on my schedule, spent the interval napping in a chair near the radiator, while her nine-year-old son, wearing the bike helmet I never saw him without, ricocheted around the room, banging into everything. "Ameenia" was the mother's explanation for his condition—nothing to do with the father and his habit of banging the boy's head against the wall. "Hemoglobina" was the solution. ("I am all day in urgency room waiting for doctor to bring blood . . . It is my fall. My fall.") I can't say our sessions made any difference, except for providing evidence for getting the father locked up and out of the way. Unfortunately, his first parole hearing would be coming round in a week or two.

For some reason, Leticia also happened to arrive early that day. She was that rarity, an almost-success story. I was hopeful for

Leticia—almost hopeful. The odds against her were formidable. Her family (so-called) was the usual welfare mess. The girl herself had been in and out of mental hospitals and drug rehab for the last two years. But, in recent months, she'd been cramming for her high school equivalency exam—exactly what she should have been doing. A model of concentration, she sat hunched forward, pencil gripped between her teeth. With her head bent severely over her book, I couldn't fail to notice the elaborate parting, braiding, and beading of her hair. How many cornrows? I wondered. And how much study time might the construction of such a hairdo consume?

Before I left the office, there was a call from Father Evans asking if I'd seen Michael; he'd failed to check in at the hostel the night before. The rule was if you have a reason for staying elsewhere, you have to call and explain. There'd been no call.

A week went by.

Three Thursdays had come and gone, and it seemed safe to say that the day of the threatened suicide had passed without mishap. There'd been nothing in the papers. It was a relief to find the suggestion box littered with the usual gripes.

That Friday afternoon, I had a long conversation with Father Evans. The gist of it was this: Michael's room was about to be assigned to another client.

"Anything you can think of, looking back, that might have triggered his walkout?" I wondered.

"You have the time?" Father Evans asked.

"Sure," I said, even though I happened to be up to my neck in monthly reports.

From what I could gather, Michael had quit his job some days before he disappeared. Typically, he'd told no one, simply cleared out his locker in the Bronx and moved all his Dumpster gleanings back into the storage room at the hostel. Father Evans—understandably—objected. There was a rule, even if the stuff had been odor-free, a five-cubic-foot limit. In most other places, the limit was far less generous. "The rule applies to everyone . . ."

He went on: Michael's stash was well over five cubic feet. Much of it was roach-laden—trash—though it would have made no difference had it been perfectly clean or contained priceless treasures. At issue was storage capacity. And—a rule was a rule. So Michael had been given three choices: paring down to meet the allowable space or renting another locker or leaving.

"Anyone offer to help him sort the stuff?" I put forward the obvious. "Weed out the stuff with roaches—"

"Wouldn't hear of it," Evans said. "He's an adult. He has to be responsible for his life. That's what we teach here."

"Any other reasons he might have bolted?" I persisted.

Father Evans paused. "Well . . ." He couldn't help noticing that Michael hadn't bonded with any of the other residents, not one, not even his roommate who'd made a special effort. "Sure," he said, "there are bound to be other reasons I don't know. God knows!— I'm not God."

A good man, Father Evans, but a brick wall sometimes. There's a brass plaque over his desk, quoting someone or other: THE FIRE LORD, NOT THE SCRAP HEAP. I've no idea what the words are supposed to mean.

"Why not give him a little more time to think it over. To reconsider," I urged.

My main concern was that he'd go off his meds. "I won't pretend I'm not worried about that," Evans said. We agreed to keep in touch and, on that inconclusive note, let the subject drop.

But, of course, the matter did not rest. I was concerned that Michael would be caught up in that all-too-familiar double bind of the homeless: no job because no address, no address because no job.

Summer evenings are sweet in the city, and lively—all that indoor life oozing out into the open. I'd wait for the asphalt to cool, leaving my office late, then set out, picking up some sort of supper on the way—a kebab or a slice of pizza. I'd play sightseer, taking in a leisurely chunk of Manhattan on my way down to the Village. Bright yellow cabs would blur past me as I strolled, but I felt no hassle, no hurry . . . it was my time to unwind. As the shadows swelled and deepened, I'd feel the knots loosen, the phantasms of the day float off into a liquid darkness.

There were always plenty of homeless out and about. Even when they rattled cups or played instruments, people tended to walk by them looking the other way, studiously not noticing.

It was on Forty-Fifth and Eighth that I spotted him—Michael— I was almost sure.

He was staring at a rather cheesy window display. A normal human bedroom, but he was gazing raptly with lips parted, as though whatever he beheld had taken his breath away. I crept up quietly and stood within yards of him, staring, trying to learn what it was that so fascinated him, but nothing in the display—the double bed with quilted cover and matching pillows in a sunburst pattern, side tables, and decorator lamps—struck me as the least bit out of the ordinary.

They ought to outlaw windows, I thought. For enticement. That bedroom scene was no part of Michael's experience, no part of the experience of any of my clientele. Most never got within touching distance.

I had all I could do to keep from speaking his name out loud. Instead, I waited, moving off only when he did. *Follow him!* I did— doing my best to keep a fixed distance. Occasionally, I'd lose sight of him and speed up.

He walked briskly, as though he had an appointment to keep, yet never forgot to jiggle the coin-return levers of any pay phones he passed along the way. It occurred to me more than once that I might be shadowing the wrong man, but the resemblance seemed striking, and I couldn't afford to let the possibility slip.

Another thing: the way he repeatedly tapped the walls of the buildings as he went by, as if to assure himself that brick and concrete continued to hold firm—I imagined this was something Michael might do.

He was carrying a large canvas shopping bag, once white maybe, now drab gray, mottled with stains. But he had no knapsack, a detail which only registered in retrospect, too late to save me from the wildest of wild goose chases as we descended from midtown on down.

We were west of Eighth Avenue, but not yet at the river, was all I knew.

. . . Kosher butcher . . . Greek deli . . . Italian grocery . . . CASA DE EMPEÑO . . . JOYERÍA . . . I couldn't take my eyes off my quarry long enough to check the street signs.

When he disappeared into an alleyway, I slowed down before turning in after him. I didn't want to lose him, but I didn't want to be trapped, either. A small crowd was gathered there.

What should I call them, those shadow people in the alley? Collectors? Recyclers? Redeemers? An enterprising group, by any standard. Two had supermarket carts. One, the only woman, fussed with a baby carriage, crammed to the top with rolls of shelf-liner and bubble wrap. Despite the heat, she was wearing two coats and a ski cap pulled down over her ears; below the first joints, her fingers were tied together with the same bright red wool as her cap. The group was clustered round an eight-foot-deep Dumpster, where one of the younger members, boosted by a stepstool, was raking the contents with a grappling hook on a long pole. He'd latched a trouble-light to the rim, too, like an auto mechanic under an open car hood. Behind him, a wheelchair in waiting and, in it, a man—dressed in jungle camouflage from some forgotten or imagined war—was killing time by beating a rat to death with a broomstick. The job was halfway done: the rat quivered but could no longer run.

The better finds were propped against the facing wall: teakettle, transistor radio, a pair of fireplace tongs, and a postage scale. A muffler. Nearby, a large, untidy heap of aluminum cans was piling up. Nothing discarded was ever really lost, I realized then; all our leavings came round.

Michael was busy at the wall, scoping out the best pickings. He stooped to examine the radio and fiddle with the dials. Nothing doing, apparently, and before long he was out of there, on his way again, heading downtown. Now and then, he'd slow up or double his pace, as if—aware of being shadowed—he wanted to shake me off, but he never once glanced back to let me know he knew.

He came to a halt in a neighborhood I didn't recognize, Puerto Rican, I guess, bodegas everywhere. Across the street, a giant crane loomed over an empty lot. I ducked into the darkened entrance of a shop.

He—the Michael person I'd been trailing—had stopped to negotiate with a man who'd spread out his merchandise curbside on a cardboard mat. Most of it, the watches, fancy sunglasses, umbrellas, and flip-flops looked to be new. Words were exchanged, watches and cash changed hands. Then, as the man with the shopping bag took off again, I did something desperate.

"Hey—wait a minute!" I called out.

He sped up—I raced after him.

I ran—ran breathlessly until close enough to stretch out my arm and tap him on the shoulder.

"You heard me!"

I snatched at his sleeve.

He shook me off. About-faced. "Who the *fuck?*"

And stared at me, snarling. Full face, I realized—he wasn't Michael. No resemblance! He was older than I'd thought, his nose different, eyes too close together—

"What's the big idea?"

Abjectly—I was too tired to care by then—I apologized: "Thought you were someone else."

"I *bet!* I could report you, you know."

I doubted he would. After all, I'd witnessed the exchange of a bunch of watches—stolen or contraband—a few blocks back. I'd seen money change hands. Yet what I'd been doing was far from innocent, if not illegal. I'd been only shadowing at first, then—stalking.

Once he was quite gone, I made my way back to the curbside merchant where he'd unloaded his goods. I felt nothing but relief to be out of hiding. By then, I was curious to get a good look at what was being offered up for sale. And what a jumble it turned out to be! Fake fashion-brand watches, matchbox cars, recycled CDs, magazines, paperbacks, ornate cut-glass doorknobs . . . A revolving spice rack—how do they call those things? Lazy-Something, a girl's name, I forget. Near the watches, a row of pens. One glowed, the top half a capsule aquarium with tiny fish flashing blue, silver, red. Fish so slight they seemed mere winks of fluorescence, the kind they called tetra—neon tetra. Twirling the pen between forefinger and thumb, the fish flurried, shimmered, looked to be swimming. I asked the seller how much, and when he said five, I started haggling: "This thing still write?"

I didn't wait for his answer but stooped down to the cardboard mat and stroked. I pressed. *Nada*. The pen was dry. I unscrewed the top. Of course!—the thing was an empty shell, there was nothing inside.

"You trying to mess with me?" It wasn't really a question. "Take it or leave it—"

I left it. Don't know why I'd even bothered. Just . . . I needed something, something tangible, to redeem the evening. But nothing else caught my eye, so I handed the pen over and started my homeward trek. What a waste of a fine evening! I'd lost my quarry, the young man who wasn't that young, who wasn't Michael. I'd lost my way, besides, and would have to take a cross-town bus to get anywhere near back on track. Hard to believe what I'd been doing. *Stalking*! What's worse, I'd been stalking the wrong person.

I wanted nothing more than to wash my mind clear of Michael then. I thought of the neon tetra pen with regret; June would have appreciated it. And then it struck me—June had owned a pen exactly like it. It had been in her handbag the day her bag was stolen; she carried it around with her because it was so hard to find a cartridge that fit. There were probably hundreds of such pens in existence, but, the fact was, I'd never seen another like it.

7

Dust

I was calm as a clock and deaf to the sound of duct tape tearing as I zoomed the vacuum around her.

Earlier that morning we'd divvied up the Sunday paper, as was our custom. To me: the book section and the summary of the week's news; to June: all the rest. The ads in the other sections—bags and baubles, scraps of cloth, sweet little nothings costing thousands—never failed to enrage me.

"Who can afford those things? No one I know."

June's answer was perfectly predictable: "You know the wrong people."

I said nothing to dispute this.

Now, having made good on her promise to pack up and leave if I walked out of her party, June was sealing boxes. She'd gathered a stash of free cartons from the liquor store on the corner. There'd been collapsible divisions inside them to keep the bottles upright and protected, which she'd left strewn all over the floor. They were neatly collapsible with only a little effort, but it was up to me to stack them and carry them out to the trash, June being much too busy to bother.

She was stooped over her books and CDs, her hair, still wet from the shower, tumbled out of its towel wrap, darker now and gleaming. Yesterday, she'd taken down the hanging pots with the bright copper backs; the wall over the stove, blank, spattered with nail holes, was a map of desolation without them. She'd sealed up the pottery mugs, the wok, and her wheel of spices. Her quilt, neatly rolled and roped, and an embroidered pillow, took up most of the coffee table. The coleus, ficus, and cactus rested in an open carton by the window. They'd been "our" plants, or so I'd told my-self, but it was probably for the best that June take them. Any growing things, even these "low maintenance" plants, were at risk in my hands—in June's considered judgment. Privately, I agreed with her.

It took me a moment to realize that I was being spoken to—or *at*. I switched off the vacuum.

"You never listen."

"I couldn't hear. Couldn't tell if you were singing or sighing—"

"Ha. Very funny," she said. "Why don't you wait till I'm out of here?" Then, muttering to herself, "I don't know why I bother . . ."

"I'll vacuum a second time. After," I promised, and I was about to press the switch again when she lurched to her feet, the better to confront me eye to eye. "Tell me something . . ."

"About what?" I knew I was in for it.

"About *me*. I keep on telling you about yourself, things you'd never notice otherwise. Things you'd better know."

June loved putting me on the spot. She's so slight, barely five feet, you'd never guess her strength, her ferocity. It's in the light-ning speed of her attack, her whipsaw judgments. What was I sup-posed to notice? Something new? Blouse? Hairdo? What if they weren't new?

"Don't make me laugh!" she said, smiling through closed lips. "How long have we lived together and you need to *think*? Then forget it. You weren't like this when we met . . ." Her stare grew hard—I wouldn't call it hateful exactly, simply opaque, stony—a gaze that gave back no rays.

Problem was I had no any energy left over for hassles at home—I used it all up at the office. If I refused to fire back at June—my usual MO—it simply went to prove that I was either (a) a passive wuss or (b) a phony saint or (c) too damned lazy to care. And wasn't it typical that I didn't even *try* to explain, choosing to let everything pass over me, letting her think anything she pleased? I couldn't win.

"Ask me why I'm leaving, Tom. Are you the least bit interested?"

I'd be damned if I spoke lines June had scripted for me, so I didn't ask. She went on, muttering to herself. "Greatest city in the world . . . might as well be living in an elevator shaft." I don't know how it happened but, at that moment, the vacuum came to life with a blast. I had no intention, it just happened—one of those little "accidents" Freud would have relished. "Whose lips are silent"—how did he phrase it?—". . . Whose lips are silent chatters with his fingertips; betrayal oozes through every pore . . ." *True, true.*

June stooped to her boxes, her mouth still working but no words coming through. I resumed my circling.

"I'll vacuum again—*after*," I said at last, though I doubted June could hear me over the roar of the machine. "Right now it gives me something to do." And besides . . . I wanted to remind her that the vacuum cleaner, a good one, was mine. It wasn't going with her.

Yet all the while I knew there was some justice in June's indictment. At home in the evening, I didn't know what to do with myself. I never wanted to go anywhere interesting, but all I did at home was sit and stew. I couldn't read, couldn't concentrate. Turning on the television (an excuse not to speak), I rarely paid attention. I didn't want to talk about my day.

Right then, I was busy making tracks. I wondered why no one had yet invented coiled cords for vacuum cleaners, like the ones on telephones. So much time and effort is wasted in plugging, unplugging, repositioning . . . And where had I read that more than 90 percent of what we think of as dust, or household dirt, is biological in nature? Offscourings: the desiccated shells of insects, pet hairs, dander, our own dandruff and fallen hair, finger and toenail parings, sloughed-off skin cells, all the constant unnoticed sheddings of our animal bodies.

I felt nothing much and thought only of petty things. Professional peeves, for one. Only yesterday morning, I'd come into my office to find my swivel chair missing. In its place: one of those comfortless, armless, wooden chairs that belong in the cubicles that pass for offices among the junior staff. Mine was one of the few padded chairs in the department, and so, a mark of status or, at least, seniority. I'd earned that chair. When I complained to Karina, she assured me that the chairs had been "accidentally switched." And truly, maybe, that's all it was, because my chair was just as mysteriously restored to me later in the afternoon. No malice intended. Karina had followed up on it and the explanation was straightforward enough: the night cleaning person, a new one, had simply been overzealous. It wasn't a slight. Why did I persist in thinking otherwise?

I hadn't realized how much I depended on that swivel for what little mobility I had, how much I depended on the support of those metal arms for what little authority I could muster.

That's what passed through my mind as I vacuumed. Anything but thinking about the person in front of me at that moment. Under the drone of the machine there was an eerie silence. No sound at all now. I circled the boxes and sucked dust, erasing June's presence, erasing June, so she could take nothing more from me . . .

Between the time June announced her decision to leave and her actual move, I had ample opportunity to recall our first meeting, to wonder what went wrong or whether we'd ever been right for one another.

She'd been on the rebound from an abusive marriage when we met and, by her own admission, lonely and scared. Lonely calls to lonely, right?

It was sheer accident that our paths ever crossed. As a rule, I can't tell instant coffee from Starbuck's finest, but this new gourmet/health grocery on Fifty-Third was offering "free gifts" as an enticement for coming in. I happened to be a sucker for freebies—it was part curiosity, part, I suspect, my larcenous heart.

So I'd gone in and, to disguise my meretricious intent, decided to investigate their coffee and even to purchase something or other so as to look like a real customer.

The free gift turned out to be a coffee mug. Completely redundant: I already had enough of a collection, most of the cups, like this one, free advertisement for one thing or another.

I was in vegetable produce, rounding the aisle, when our paths quite literally crossed—our carts collided. When I backed off to let her pass, I couldn't help noticing what she'd picked out. I recognized only the bok choy, the white radish, the chards, and the red cabbage. The rest—heaps of roots I couldn't identify, and assorted grasses—was topped by what looked like a giant fungus. I have no first impression of June herself; what captured my attention were the vegetation and, above all, the fungus.

Nothing further came of our first meeting, but I did start dropping in at that shop from time to time. It was the kind of gourmet place I'd always dismissed as overpriced and much too yuppie, and there I was stopping by for halvah or macadamia nuts or figs from Smyrna or some other contrived need. The second time I ran into June, I invited her out for coffee afterward. Pure whim on my part, and I almost misheard her assent: I hadn't really expected her to take me up on it. She wasn't coy, nor did she sound overly enthusiastic, she was simply willing to give it a go. I liked that.

But she had to deposit her groceries first. Said she lived "nearby." She was prudently vague on exactly where that was, though she promised it would take no more than ten minutes going and coming. I agreed to find us a table at the Greek place across the street. We ordered spinach pie and green tea and settled down to the standard preliminaries of getting acquainted—ages, hometowns, jobs, hobbies, pet peeves, favorite things . . . I can't say either of us was, then or ever, swept away; we'd both been around the block too many times for that. But the vibes between us were warm, the timing was right. I found her frankness, her no-nonsense briskness, refreshing at first, then bracing, little suspecting how abrasive it might become. I was partial to her smile, her delicate ears, and the color of her eyes—bright blue, a cornflower blue. I've always imagined blue eyes to be more intelligent than brown (my own color). I noticed that we were well sized for one another, our bodies would fit. It seemed enough to build on. She must have thought so, too. And we'd had our season.

Sympathetic magic, maybe: there was a downpour on the Saturday morning June actually left—the world weeping for one who could not, and one who would not, weep. For purely practical reasons, I considered urging June to postpone the move until the heavy weather lifted then thought the better of it. What would be the point in dragging this out? Why prolong the pain? So I raised no objection. Said nothing. For the past week we'd made a game, it seemed, of hurting one another. June was in a hurry to get away, I—to get it over with.

And, like a good tenant clearing her accounts, June insisted on relinquishing her house keys. A studied gesture, she'd placed them between the silver candlesticks on the dining room table. Those candlesticks, a wedding present to my parents, were a piece of inheritance, my only heirloom. June had resurrected them from a battered suitcase in my closet and scoured all their blackness away. I still don't know what possessed her. Marriage was never an issue between us; we'd both been married before and, once-burned, were twice-shy on that score.

I insisted she keep her own set of keys. "In case you've left something behind."

"Couldn't be anything important, I've checked," she said.

"Keep them anyway. A souvenir."

She pocketed the keys. We stood in the ravaged living room at a loss for words.

Earlier, she'd dismantled the standing lamp, packed away the Navajo rug, and scrolled up the Miró poster. You could see exactly where the poster had been hanging, a ghost-trace of its presence, milk white, against the yellowed wall.

"Well . . . Got to go," she said.

There were no closing arguments. There was nothing new to be said. June had been diligent in keeping me up-to-date on her ever-lengthening list of grievances. Item: my lack of attention: "Present in body, absent in spirit," my mind always elsewhere. Case in point: a kitchen knife she'd found stabbed to the hilt in a block of soap. I could have explained, but what would be the use? I'd mistaken the soap for tofu, extra-firm—what was soap doing in the food pantry in the first place? But, to June, the stabbing spoke for itself of hostility I refused to acknowledge. Item: my indifference to the little things that made life sweet, like conversation, recreation, holidays, and special occasions such as birthdays. (That luncheon again when I didn't show up and her purse was stolen.) Item: my refusal to join a squash club. Item: my inability to sit through anything on television except for breaking news, and, nine times out of ten, breaking news, as everyone knows, means disaster . . . The conclusion struck June as inescapable: "Get a life, Tom. You're depressed." And my greatest failing, since inclusive of the rest: "Refusing professional help. You, of all people."

Preparing to escort June as far as I could, I took an umbrella with me. From the foyer, I could make out someone double-parked alongside a fire hydrant out in front. Inside the van: the clumped shadow of a man who remained featureless—the windows were too steamed. I hesitated on the dry side of the final door, my hand on the knob.

"Don't," she urged, "don't come. No point both of us getting soaked." She shook her head. "You are so fucked up," she said softly, and I thought I heard a touch of tenderness in it.

Then I sideswiped a kiss, on her cheek. Never made it to her lips. She opened the door a crack; the rain beat down, unabated.

"Well, June, it's—" My throat seized.

The words I managed after that startled us both:

"It's been fun."

Bad situation! I tried to explain. "Look, I didn't mean . . . anything. It's this itch I get in my throat—" but June's face was already turned away; I could see it was useless.

The words, once out, could not be unsaid.

8

Stone City

"Want to explain what's been going on?"

He mumbled something about a stomachache, it being somebody else's stomach or somebody else's problem, or something—I wasn't listening properly—I had no patience for excuses.

"We're not here to talk about the weather," I said.

I was unprepared for Michael's reappearance and never would have expected he'd be on time for his appointment, too. But he was deathly pale, his voice threadlike. Standing, he clutched my desk for support—like an old man.

In fact, he'd been hospitalized. That no one on the hospital staff had informed Father Evans or myself struck me as inexcusable. I could easily imagine how it happened, though, with Michael too far gone to name his contacts and his IDs left back at the hostel.

He'd been unconscious when the police picked him up off the street. One of his favorite Dumpsters had been doused with rat poison. He could have died.

True to form, he tried to dismiss the incident. "I've always been lucky," he began.

Not even he could miss the stony silence with which I greeted this remark.

"I learned my lesson," he amended.

"Oh, yeah . . . And what lesson was that?"

"Be care-ful!" he recited, and went on to give a note-perfect rendition of someone telling him what he was supposed to say: "I wasn't being careful like I need to be. Looking out for food that's too old. Making sure the air seal isn't broken."

"It's not enough to be careful—it has to stop! *You* have to stop!"

My voice was shaking.

I took a deep breath and started over, trying to reason with him. "You've got to quit. You're not dumb. It doesn't matter whether the seal is broken or not, or whether the date on the outside is past or still okay. What difference can it make when the Dumpster is full of poison? You nearly died of rat poisoning, and there's only one lesson to be learned from it: Quit eating out of Dumpsters! You can't trust any of it."

"It wasn't her doing—" The words startled us both.

"*Her* doing?" I knew that I'd stumbled onto something.

"She wouldn't throw potato salad into a paper bag like that. Like trash—"

"It *is* trash! If not rat poison, it'd be rat droppings—they can be every bit as lethal."

I had all I could do to keep from shouting.

Then, suddenly, I backed up. "Who's this *she?*"—the first I'd heard of any female in his life.

No answer, of course. *Of course.* It was too important a question.

Once again, I was living alone. Looking back, it occurred to me that June hadn't even bothered to create a scene at the end. You know how it is when two lie in silence, side by side yet beyond reach, in the same bed, a mere hand-span of air between them—unbridgeable. We were past talking, even arguing; nothing seemed worth arguing by then. It was the nothing that weighed and sickened.

June had walked out once before this but, then, for days afterward I'd keep finding things she'd forgotten to take along. I had reason to think this time was different: she'd left so little behind. The mailbox, too, was empty of her presence; she must have made arrangements for forwarding well in advance.

I was a bit surprised then by June's stopping by less than a month after her departure. "To look for my watch," her excuse. She'd telephoned beforehand, although I reminded her that wasn't necessary—she still had her own key. Together we stooped under the couch and the bed, stirring up a lot of dust, and emptying the medicine cabinet, which needed sorting in any case. The watch failed to turn up.

"I don't know why I was making such a fuss over it. It was only a Timex."

"But those are the best kind," I said, raising my wrist and tapping my own, which happened to be a gift from her.

"I guess I had a sort of sentimental attachment . . ."

"To a watch, nothing else?" I couldn't resist.

"Don't press, Tom."

I didn't. We stepped warily around each other, an intricate dance. I offered her a drink, a bite to eat . . .

"Let's not start being polite to each other at this late date," she declared. "I know perfectly well where things are."

"Now that you mention it, you did leave a thing or two in the fridge—that miso base and those unpronounceable plums."

"Oh my gosh, my umeboshi plums! How could I forget?" She was on her feet instantly.

I followed. She dove straight for the plums then backed up clutching the jar to her chest.

"Sure you'd never touch them?"

"Not on your life." I'd tasted them once, those salty, pickled, unpronounceable plums. "Don't forget that other jar behind it."

She parked her jars on the counter and made for the cupboard.

"Oh, and my twig tea!"

I'd assumed June's passion for macrobiotics was waning, but I wasn't up on the latest, and bit my tongue to avoid tangling on a touchy subject. I'd come to learn only lately that she'd been an anorexic for years, then a convert (but this I'd known) and the fiercest of proselytizers for one food fad after another. Her macrobiotic efforts had been utterly wasted on me. She'd posted warning signs on the cupboard doors under the headings EXTREME YIN and EXTREME YANG, foods to be avoided. I ate too much of one or the other, imbalance was my problem, a tendency to extremes. I made no effort to solve my problem, refused to concede any problem existed. Tape marks from her postings were still evident, though she'd taken the signs down weeks ago.

While I ferreted around for a bag for her, I knew June was taking stock. Sure enough, the next thing she said was, "I see you finally got the microwave you wanted."

"Finally, yes. I zap everything."

"As if you're pressed for time." The argument was old, old.

"Better things to do with whatever time I've got."

"Such as—?" It went on like this, pointless.

I'd thought our conversational possibilities exhausted, but when we made our way to the living room she surprised me by sitting back down.

"How's it going? How are you?"

How was I? "Yangy, or is it yingy? The usual." As usual, I made a joke of it. She could see for herself—crumbs on the couch, takeout cartons in the fridge, a thin fur of dust on everything.

But *she* looked fine; I assured her I wasn't being polite in saying this. She was wearing a velour outfit, matching wine-colored sweater and slacks, very flattering. The entire ensemble seemed to be new, but I'd never paid enough attention to be sure of these things, and I didn't risk commenting, knowing I'd be in for it, deep and deeper, if it turned out to be something she'd worn on and off for years. Surely, though, the belt was new, the fact that she was wearing a belt, a silvery belt, cinching her waist, *that* was new. For whose benefit? I was itching to ask but, wisely, once again I squelched it.

She was busier than ever at the office these days. Not much life left over, she had to admit. She'd seen the dangers of allowing this to happen in my own case, but it was the only way she was able to keep up.

Not a peep from me.

June was a paralegal for a big corporate law firm on Park Avenue at the time. She'd been saving up, hoping to make enough to start law school. She'd make a good prosecuting attorney, I'd come to think. She called me a "bleeding heart"—I called that ridiculous. If I really were a bleeding heart, would I have lasted out even a month at the kind of work I do? Fat chance.

"What's new with Michael?" she asked suddenly.

"Nothing. Still hanging out around Dumpsters, I'm afraid."

"Why Dumpsters?"

I shrugged.

"For no reason? Got to be a reason."

I tried to think of one. It was true: no one, not even a person we call "mentally ill," lives in randomness. "It's the only constant thing in his record, hanging around Dumpsters" was the best I could come up with.

"Maybe something he lost? Must be hoping to find something."

"Food." But I knew that wasn't the whole story.

"That can't be all," she said.

"Why not? You, of all people! Guess you've never been *really* hungry. Food—and half the time it's rotten!"

"Eat the worm and get the vision."

"Ha," I said.

"Hey, I'm joking," she said, "can't you take a joke? It's what they say about tequila . . . Forget it. You were saying?"

"What he's looking for . . . Food, first and foremost. What else? A lucky find—some castoff clothing, maybe. He'd have no use for furniture. What else could there be?"

"A connection."

"You mean drugs? There's nothing in his file—"

"Who said anything about drugs?"

I didn't let on about the mysterious female whom Michael had mentioned some sessions back but never once after that. June had spoken more presciently than she knew.

Before she left, we said the good-byes appropriate to out-of-towners meeting on a street corner: "Keep in touch," she said—or I said.

We promised to keep in touch.

Fall arrived and Michael disappeared again; fall settled in; not a trace. The nights fell earlier, grew longer, colder. You had to assume that the people who persisted in living out on the streets didn't feel it anymore—not like the rest of us, anyway.

I contacted Dr. Kirsch, who sounded not at all surprised. "He's good for two refills on his last prescription—a recent one; he could, conceivably, get by for as long as three months. That's *if* he continues taking his meds. Big assumption! Some patients stretch their meds for a couple of months by taking less than prescribed. I don't think there's anything on chart for him you don't already have. I don't think he's a danger to anyone else . . ."

I kept in touch with Father Evans: no news there. I urged him to keep the door open for Michael should he turn up and want to start over. Greeted with silence, I pleaded, "Is there no right of appeal? No second chance?"

"We're not here to foster dependency" was Father Evans's official line (same as ours), but right before hanging up, he softened: "Michael has to show up first. First things first."

I knew next to nothing and yet, at the same time—go figure!—despite my long training and repeated warnings from counseling texts, I'd managed to get myself "personally involved." But there were reasons . . . I once heard a colleague mention an "unfinished task syndrome," a subspecies of obsessive compulsive disorder. Maybe that was what drove me, for I wasn't done with Michael. In truth, I'd barely begun.

I did try to let go, reminding myself that Michael was only one of countless missing in the city. It didn't help. My life outside the office being what it was—a shambles—clearly had a part to play in my fixation, obsession over a recalcitrant case offering distraction from my own woes.

❖

54

Wednesday morning I was hailed by a man standing on the curb, staring at the street in front of my apartment building.

"Somebody living under there," he pointed.

"What makes you think?"

"Why they call it a manhole," and he laughed. "I seen food and stuff disappear down that hole. It's a nice setup, actually, snug, pretty safe." He took a few steps out into the road, stomped twice on the thick steel cover, and shouted to the ground, "Hey, there!"

"Why doesn't he come out?"

"He must, I guess. Least I hope he does. When nobody's looking maybe. But, see, the other side of the cover says KEEP OUT—the guys from Transportation forgot to turn it over when they finished working down there."

Long story short: When the Transportation Department crew closed the hatch, the writing on the cover was facing inside. So whoever's hiding down under there must think it's the world up top he's been warned not to enter.

He'd be a bag of bones by now, I thought.

Too much! What I needed, I decided, was a breather. I had to get away—anywhere—out of the city. Couple of days might do the trick. But soon. Before I, too—

9

Clear Air Turbulence

Needing that breather I mentioned, it seemed an opportune time to accept my sister's invitation to come out for Thanksgiving. It had been a while. The year of Mom's death, I made a point of making the trip to Nan's home in Los Angeles twice, but since then, it had dwindled down to once every two or three years. I fully expected that my nephew and niece would be less than overjoyed to see me this time. I'd been keen on them when they were kids; they were imaginative and loving, cuddly as kittens. The youngest, Leo, used to rush out the door to be the first to greet me, shouting, "I carry you!" meaning exactly the reverse, and I'd feel this huge, undeniable burst of joy as I lifted him, but, even then, I knew that I couldn't count on it to last—kittens, alas, become cats. I consoled myself with the thought that, even if I had been more diligent about keeping up, the kids, along with all their preadolescent cohorts, were bound to be out of reach by now. As for Nan and her husband, Lenny, they were nice enough, couldn't be nicer, really. We'd never had that much in common, though; that hadn't changed, and maybe that's why they'd invited an additional person (about which not a word was said beforehand.) Then again, I suspect Nan was the one behind the scheme, her motive all too obvious. Had I mentioned my break-up with June? But I'm getting ahead of myself here—

To begin with, I've always been a nervous flyer. I'm never eager to travel. Even the smoothest flight—and except for one patch of clear air turbulence around Phoenix, this one was smooth and uneventful—makes me feel like I'm jumping out of my skin. As soon as I'm strapped in, squinching the seat belt extra tight, palpating the locked and upright tray table with a doubting hand, as soon as we start streaking down the runway, my heart stampedes. I try to get a grip on myself, I do, clenching my teeth, bearing down on the armrests, holding on for dear life as we thunder past. The last runway markers melt into the earth—I can't for an instant let go.

Then liftoff—the disconnect.

I feel it, the soles of my feet feel it: the floor floats, no ground beneath—we're leaving earth behind.

It's no better at cruising altitude: cars, matchbook houses, factories dwindled to specks, to less than specks; roads and rivers vanished, whited-out. I never grow accustomed, never find rest in the flow, but continue to sit in straight-back position, rigid yet quaking. I sweat, the portholes hum and sweat, framing cloud flash, jet flash, a great sea of burning blue. I never chat with my neighbor, never open the tray table to receive the complimentary beverage to which I'm entitled. The pilot drones on, broadcasting—something—a joke? a weather note?—something I don't catch, for, through his voice, his studied monotone, I hear the monster engines seethe. Attendants smile and nod, receiving the drink orders, bowing to everyone's least wishes. I have this overwhelming urge to rip the oxygen masks out from their cubbies hidden behind the light panels. Let them dangle down in readiness, in plain sight! Let's quit pretending now. The signals to fasten/unfasten seat belts come in triplets, cheery-bright; I never unfasten my seat belt, the little bells ting in vain. So much show-tuned niceness and I am undeceived: We are doomed. Insubstantial as cloud shadows dappling the earth. Were we ever real?

Only after the recoil of touchdown—after the shuddering grinding groaning blasting—flung down, poured out, rejoined with the living stream, I'm overcome with gratitude. If the cockpit door is open, I lean in to thank the pilot and copilot. I thank the attendants. Profusely. I all but kneel and kiss the earth. I am, for the moment at least, cleansed of all meanness—generous, welcoming, and kind. It never lasts, of course. Before I know it, I'm mired in all the usual small and petty, earthbound detail.

And so it was this time . . . I was greeted enthusiastically by Nan and even more lavishly by Rosalind, her overfed miniature pug, who serves as hostess, centerpiece, and conversational crutch. The two of them led me out to the deck where the others were gathered.

"Hey, Tom!" Lenny pummeled my shoulder. "Still saving the world, one client at a time?" to which I replied, "I *wish!*" for I was learning to parry remarks like this. We embraced: big A-frame hug with back-patting. I gave as good as I got, pat for pat, trying to impersonate the close buddies we'd never been. The kids, Janie and Leo, were too busy squabbling over a video camera to do more than scope me out from the surrounding greenery. I went through the obligatory "my, how they've grown!" for their parents' sake.

And then there was Valerie. Anytime people try to match me up, it's doomed from the start. Nan knows this, or *should*. I'd warned her, time and time again, not to try and balance genders—not to set me up. I much prefer asymmetry: I'm much more comfortable being the odd man out. Nan knew this.

Poor Valerie . . . We did the rote: Where-do-you? How-long-have-you? and might have gone on to birthdays and favorite colors if nothing else had presented itself. But then, suddenly—it did. Turned out that Valerie was in recovery from a recent divorce. What a coincidence! She must have been as unaware of Nan's set-up beforehand as I'd been—I'll give her the benefit of the doubt. Something, I suppose, might have been built on our shared embarrassment, had either of us been inclined. She was wearing open sandals with thin braided straps, and whenever the conversation sagged, I stared at her feet, struck by the lift, the tease, the tense backward flexion of her big toes. All my neuroticisms must have been in full flower then, to feel so unnerved—unmanned, really—

by the sight of those upthrusting toes. Unnerved and at the same time fascinated—it required a concerted effort to release my gaze and shift it elsewhere. There we were, basking in the sun, the redwood deck overgrown with lush, fringed, and possibly fanged vegetation, with splashes of green, pink, and crimson—bougainvillea, bottle-brush, hundreds of blooming things whose names I'd never learn. Slugging beer, with our recliner chairs tilted way back, we must have looked like a scene in one of those glitzy travel ads for California. The air was exceptionally clear: you didn't often get that kind of visibility in L.A. You could actually make out a patch of the Pacific down in the distance.

I should explain: Nan and Lenny lived "in the hills," their house braced on stilts. "Up on poles, like a birdhouse," I liked to tease. They weren't that far from the HOLLYWOOD sign, and only a few tiers above the house where Rudolph Valentino's last mistress lived until quite recently. Her house was a major topic of conversation. Built to custom for the lady, ages ago, it was still languishing on the market, still overpriced and in dire need of repair. People pretending to be potential buyers flocked to the place out of curiosity, hoping to gawk at the still-breathing mummy, who sat in silence, costumed to the nines, planted on the living room couch, or, in her absence, at least to eyeball the living room portraits of the famous lovers embracing in their palmier days.

I was so not-interested it was bound to show. Nan, moving continually to and fro from the kitchen, tried to discourage me from tagging after her, insisting that I "just sit. Relax. Try to decompress. Plenty of time for catching up later." I promised to return to the fray, but first I wanted to look around. There'd been a few changes since my last visit.

It's a lovely house. Really. I complimented Nan on all they'd done by way of upkeep and renovation. They'd added a sunroom and a small shed out back to relieve household clutter. And they'd converted part of the garage to a pottery studio. (Nan's hobby had turned a small profit this year.) The studio wasn't spacious, but serviceable enough.

I knew better than anyone how much having a house meant

to Nan. When she was a kid, especially after Dad died, we moved around so often. One apartment after another and, moving in or out, you could never tell who'd been living there. We were faceless tenants, birds of passage, who left no traces. So Nan would scribble her name on the wall, in some corner of her bedroom, behind a piece of furniture. Mom went ballistic at moving time when the writing came to light, afraid that it would be used as a reason for not refunding our security deposit, causing the forfeit of a full month's rent. This actually happened, but just the once. It was only gradually that I came to see Nan's gesture as anything but destruction. It was preservation—self-preservation.

Lenny and Valerie were still at it, talking shop, dropping names, when I rejoined them. They were both "in the Industry," as they say in L.A.: she a set dresser, he a sound engineer. They'd worked together on a number of films at one of the big studios.

The kids were up and down, video camera forgotten. Then they were busy with their cell phones, which kept them hopping, stepping away from us, clapping their free ears shut. "They ought to graft those things directly onto the ear," Lenny observed, "and palm pilots right into the palm. Maybe someday . . ." I said something inane about the time not being far off, simply to prove I'd been listening.

There was a party going on next door, a Hawaiian theme, and for a while I zoned out on their music. Then, having nothing better to do, I roused myself, ambled to the edge of Nan's deck, and peered over the railing. They'd rigged up a rough platform of leftover lumber for a stage. On it, a lovely girl, with a white flower wreath in her long streaming hair, and flower circlets round her ankles, was swaying to the sound of a boom box. A live drummer standing behind her kept rhythm to her undulations. The girl was wearing nothing but a sarong, which she kept tugging down away from her waist to reveal a generous swell of hip. What looked to be a pair of salad bowls, tied in a halter arrangement, covered her breasts. She moved as though through water; her hands, in liquid placations of the air, stroked from side to side.

No one seemed to be paying attention to the entertainment,

though. Most of the adults were busy stuffing themselves at the buffet, and the kids, in a flurry of balloons and bubbles, were jostling for a place on the trampoline out on the lawn.

"What's all that about?" I turned to Lenny.

"Next door, you mean? An aloha party. It's the kid's birthday."

"How old?" I wondered.

"Two."

Only in California, I thought. And apropos of that, I recalled Lenny having a colleague in special effects conjure up a white Christmas when the kids were younger—fake snow artfully disposed over their roof and lawn. That's not how the rest of us do on planet earth, I'm afraid.

But I held my peace.

When Nan returned to the kitchen with Lenny in tow, I was left in the company of Valerie and Rosalind. Perhaps I overdid the petting out of sheer nervousness—before I knew it, the creature was in my lap, her nose rooting around in my crotch with such single-minded enthusiasm, I had to call for someone to come rescue me.

"Sorry about that," Lenny said, giving her a whack. "She has this thing about crotches. Certain body parts like between the toes—another favorite."

She'd left an all-too-visible damp spot the size of my full hand on the front of my trousers. Lenny offered to lend me a pair of his jeans. He's a good deal taller than I am, but I could have rolled them up. He offered a pair of shorts. But I never wear shorts. So I went around the next several hours looking like I'd pissed myself.

There was a fresh stab at conversation. About New York, about my job, welfare, street crime, subway crime . . . "I don't know how you stand it, all those deadbeats—" Lenny blurted.

I couldn't let that pass. "Yes, and how about all those ARMED RESPONSE signs on the gates of houses here in L.A.?"

Lenny changed the subject quickly enough. (They have such a sign on their own gate.) Trying to tone it down a bit, I contrived something about the homeless in L.A. seeming more cheerful than the New York variety, and I mentioned one man I'd glimpsed in a brightly colored jester's cap, with dangling lappets and jingle bells, trudging along Sunset Boulevard. It was my best effort, and a lame one, prompting Nan to go fetch the photo album—always a distraction and a bid for family harmony. We leaned over the pages, Nan translating for Valerie: "There's our mom in one of her silly hats . . . That's Mom pushing the stroller . . . That's me and Tom at Halloween, must've been ages ago. I was a princess. What were you, Tom? Superman, I'd guess from your black cape, but you're not wearing the big 'S' so I don't know . . ."

I couldn't, for the life of me, recall. The trip down memory lane continued: "Not too original, anyhow . . . This one must've been Christmas—Rosalind in her Santa hat. She was only a couple months old—"

There were some new additions; the kids had discovered a bunch of photos yellowed with age in a shoebox up in the attic, and Nan had added a number of pages. *What have we here?* I wondered, fixing on a picture I'd never seen before. I recognized Eddie at once despite the fact that the few photos of him I'd ever been shown must have been taken under protest—they were so unfocused. I was five when he vanished; you'd think there'd be more of a memory trace. I got his room afterward, for the first time space to myself, although his favorite things were everywhere. I was supposed to inherit his clothes as well, but someone advised my mother that dressing me in his hand-me-downs wasn't such a good idea. The clothes were bundled off to charity long before I was able to fill them, so I pictured them as huge and Eddie himself as grown outsized in death.

I couldn't recall Eddie's face or the sound of his voice, yet the boy in the photograph was unmistakable. The focus was sharp: he was wearing shorts and a striped jersey and clutching a toy airplane. Scuffed, knobby knees, one sneaker unlaced. Cowlick. Nothing out of the ordinary in any of this . . . but he was terribly thin, and there was something—a rigidity—the tightness of his grip on the toy, as if someone nearby had made a grab for it. He was staring point-blank at the camera, at the viewer, his gaze frozen—impenetrable, yet penetrating, I felt. Same as when someone blind turned clouded eyes to fix on me—the eerie sense that he looked not at but clear *through* me.

There was another picture, unmistakably Eddie, though this one looked like a double exposure at first; then I figured he must have been turning his face—fast—his head so blurred with motion it seemed wrapped in light. He was hitting a bush with a stick, a flowering bush. "Who is it?" I asked. But, of course, I knew I knew.

"That one? Three guesses. I'd say he was eight or nine there."

"I always wondered what he died of."

"Not sure Mom and Dad ever knew."

"Never knew? Or never told?"

"He suffered from asthma. But why stir all that up? I don't know —no one ever said."

"I seem to remember something like . . . a trapeze . . . in his room."

"You couldn't possibly!" Nan insisted. "You were much too young. What's the *point?*"

What *was* it I remembered? I recalled little else with the same clarity except for his once telling me that he had a mushroom growing between his legs. He made me promise to keep it secret, and I did—I never told.

"Don't go there—" and the page was turned. "Get a look at this, will you? Isn't it a hoot?"

It was a First Communion picture from back in the days when few families had cameras of their own. A group photo, formal, stiff. A priest hovered off to one side. The children stood in a black-and-white trapezoid formation: two rows of dark-suited boys, the girls in white dresses a long line in front. They stood in replicate: faces full front, elbows wide, palms pressed together, fingers steepled under their chins, the girls' stick legs aligned as neatly as pickets in a fence. Except for this one girl standing with her legs crossed, her legs so tightly pressed together that you had to look twice to be able to make it out. At shoe level, you couldn't miss it: She was standing on reversed feet, her legs crossed in a wildly contorted posture that, once noticed, spoiled the effect of the entire composition. The girl's face looked vaguely familiar.

"That Mom?" It seemed a safe-enough guess.

Nan nodded. "Who else! Looks like somebody keeping her fingers crossed when everyone else is giving the victory salute, she's jinxing the whole deal. When I turned the picture over to check it out, sure enough, she'd written, "Me—third from left.""

"She always did have a weak bladder . . . It seems pretty obvious," I added, "that her mind was entirely elsewhere. Whatever was supposed to happen spiritually on that occasion never did happen."

"Could be something planted and passed on to the next generation," Nan said. "Like a recessive gene. You live like a monk, after all . . ."

That did it!

I clapped the album shut. End of subject—but I knew my face was blazing. Nan was fishing for a denial, for an update on my love life or a public confession of need; I wasn't about to give her the satisfaction.

All through the afternoon and evening, one photo above all, that quickly banished glimpse of my brother Eddie as a child—the sadness, the tightness—stayed with me.

They took pictures of the feast. Or, rather, Valerie did. I offered but Nan wouldn't have it, insisting that the whole point was to get me in as part of the family for a change. So there (minus Valerie) we all were, complete with turkey and trimmings. Lenny was toasting the main course, Nan passing the gravy boat in my direction. I was making some point or other, wagging a drumstick like a plump, monitory finger. The kids were already digging in, yams studded with marshmallows heaped high on their platters. Everyone smiling, or making an effort to. We all had red eyes from the flash. I had no idea how fast my hair was thinning.

I stayed overnight but couldn't sleep much. Only toward morning was I able to catch a few winks. I remember one dream. I was carrying a live bundle on my back: a child whose face I never saw, a child who grew heavier and heavier until I stumbled and threw him off. I was awakened by the sound of something on the roof. It must have been a bird scratching on the tiles, calling "kee-kiddies! k-kiddies!"—making it impossible to fall back to sleep. Morning broke cold and wet; there was no dawn. And no one stirring except that demented bird, calling "k-kiddies!"—but fainter now, farther off.

Things started to come back after this, slippery traces of images I couldn't be sure I'd seen or interpreted rightly. I recalled strained whispers, knob-rattling, heads bent to the keyhole, supper plates growing cold on the floor, offerings to a door that would not open. That was Eddie's bedroom, which I inherited, where it *seemed* to me (for, as Nan said, I was too young to understand) he'd disappeared for months on end before he disappeared for good. Then, when the room became mine, before it was plastered over, I remembered strange dents and gouges in the wall, hieroglyphs I tried, but never managed, to make sense of.

So much is dark, still.

Before I took off, Lenny shunted me aside. "Nan's concerned," he confided. "Looks like you lost a little weight . . ." Now *he* was fishing. Of course, Nan must have put him up to it. She didn't want to pry, but—

"Not to worry," I assured him. I knew where this was leading. With few opportunities to confront me face-to-face, Nan had aired her concern by e-mail and telephone. Her fear was that I'd never grow up and, at the same time, that I was becoming a prematurely old man. "So which is it?" I'd chide, she had to make up her mind. Doddering or never matured? But I knew what worried her: everyone else had changed, grown, moved on; I, alone, seemed to be stalled.

I agreed not to let so much time pass before my next visit, a promise easily made, for the possibility of future travel—the future itself—hardly seemed credible to me at that moment. Although the sun was shining on my departure, the winds light, I was already in panic mode, thinking in histrionic terms (*spinning in air . . . no ground beneath*), dreading the long flight back.

10

Deafly

Gary was talking at last, telling me about the dream he'd had the night before, how he'd been shot between the eyes, how "wonderful" it felt, then, still smiling, why his hospital therapy hadn't worked out. I reminded myself to listen hard to the words, his actual words, but the hectic glitter in his eye spoke even more insistently: he was *using* again. Then, too, the twinkling of an earring, a single earring, zircon or glass or diamond chip, added to the distraction. The earring was something new . . . Signifying what? Gay or straight? Depended on whether right ear or left . . . (Left, in Gary's case.) But which was which? And wasn't there a way of signaling that he was going steady or still looking around? Some time back, I'd jotted down a bunch of markers like these for future reference, but now, when the notes would have been helpful, I couldn't recall a thing beyond the fact that I had, indeed, drawn up such a list . . . Another thing: Did he keep the pinky nail on his right hand so much longer than the others for a reason? Was he back on cocaine, using that nail as a spoon? I considered the feverish tempo of his speech, the amped-up wattage of his smile. Where to begin?

Start with what he just said. Something about a dance, a hoedown . . .

"Doing the hokey pokey, you and you and you and you—everybody—gotta jump in. Assholes! They think they're alive."

"Say what? Hokey?" Once again, busy reminding myself to pay attention, to concentrate, I'd blinked and—a second is all it took—I'd lost the thread. Luckily, this time, Gary put the best possible spin on the situation.

"*You* don't know," he brightened, "even you! Everybody knows that shit—you make a big circle and 'you put your right foot in, you take your right foot out, and you do the hokey pokey and twirl yourself about—"

"Good grief . . ." I commiserated.

"You put your *left* foot in . . ."

Once started, there was no stopping him. I waited through hands, right and left, Gary's voice mounting to a near-hysterical pitch. "You put your *whole self* in! You take your whole self out! Do the hokey pokey! That's what it's all about!"

Gary leaned back finally as if to say, "I rest my case." Then, as was his habit, he reached for his meager ponytail, lifting it over his head and twisting it into a rope, all the while grasping the twist so tightly that his knuckles blanched; and when it snaked out of his hand, he started the whole business over again. There's a name for this: "choreiform motion," if I'm not mistaken; but naming didn't explain a thing. And his muttering "I don't like to be jerked around!" as he yanked his own hair made no sense at all.

After that he tried to explain why he couldn't eat sitting across from his best (and, I suspect, only) friend. "I reach for a fork and—his head falls off." He gave me a hard stare as he said this to let me know he wasn't joking.

"Really?"—my lame reply—"Sure he wasn't just nodding?"

"That's what *you* say." He regarded me without blinking, this hard, blistering stare. I did my best to meet it with a steady, level gaze. He made a visor of his hand and lowered his eyes. "It's your glasses—too many rays!"

Have I mentioned that I wear glasses? Often, I place them on the desk (resting my eyes or, calculatedly, trying to project a "deep," confiding, unprotected look); afterward, I spend more time than I can afford searching for them.

"I see rays, and faces—whole mob of fucking smiley faces."

To be obliging, I removed my glasses, folded the stems, and placed them carefully, mindfully, up against the phone.

That wasn't what he meant of course, not at all. He wanted my attention, my undivided attention, and what he was getting was intermittent and flickering at best. I should have recognized this during our last session when I'd stolen a glance at my wrist (a hint of time-keeping, even though I'd forgotten to put on my watch), and he'd flown into a rage. But, whatever I'd failed to notice in the past, I knew I was missing a golden opportunity right then. In other hands, this might have been a breakthrough moment. Causing a friend's head to fall off by reaching for a fork—so clear an example of how he projected his aggression onto others—wasn't likely to present itself anytime soon. Yet, somehow, the effort, the energy, needed for follow-through seemed beyond me at that moment, my heart simply not in it.

One other thing: before he got up to leave, he said in a voice so diminished it was almost a whisper, "I could live in your closet if you'd let me . . ."

"You're not serious," I said.

"I was, but I'm not now."

Then I noticed that his hands were trembling.

Gary remained a puzzle to me. Never sure when it was fun and games with him or when in earnest, I failed to credit clear warning signs. Maybe it was his background: drug and alcohol (or "pot and porn" as he chose to call it), not my specialty and a world for which I've never had much sympathy. Here he was in front of me—literally, "in my face"—and I found it hard to keep the man in focus. It was the one who got away who preyed on my mind.

I knew full well that there were other things going on in the world. I read the newspaper faithfully, but my eye invariably gravitated to the dire, the deeply troubling, in the midst of so much else. I read in one gulp, for it confirmed my worst suspicions, a story about apartment dwellers dying alone in the greatest city in the world; people, mainly elderly ("social death preceding biological death" according to the eminent sociologist consulted), decomposing in isolation, their bodies seeping into their rugs, slowly weeping through the ceilings of the apartments beneath, only noticed weeks afterward by neighbors troubled by the stench . . . Of course, there were plenty of other doings, treaties and weddings, concerts, lotteries and prizes, and other people—*happy people!*—but the upbeat rarely caught my eye and never left a lingering impression. I tried, really tried, to keep the larger picture ever in view; the television kept me up on events of the day from all corners of the world. Although my attention was sure to wander, the major stories were so often repeated that I pieced them together eventually; there was little I missed. My favorite was CNN with its never-flagging excitement of "breaking news": pet rescues, live abductions, pandas mating in captivity, famine, fashion, suicide bombings in full glorious color viewed from the coziness of my La-Z-Boy. A special feature on eating disorders—too much, too little, too faddish—rampant in the U.S. I scanned the local news, the crowds milling around any disaster scene, people standing and rubbernecking, or scurrying, always on the lookout for one in particular, lost in the common element, his difference imperceptible to others, but glaring to me.

I spent more time than ever at home but could not settle.

The television was a constant presence. I kept it on for the same reason people have pets, or keep a fire going—to feel something alive and moving in an otherwise empty room. I welcomed the theme music for the primetime evening news, a loud, beating pulse not my own, greeted the anchors as old familiars, almost friends, and reveled in talking heads with overlapping voices—what they called a "debate"—a feeding frenzy in which the loudest, fastest, gobbled up the rest.

Late nights, when I couldn't fall asleep, when I'd weary of my own "thoughts" (reruns and test patterns mostly), my hand would reach for the remote—it was rarely far from me—and I entered a world that never slept. I'd marvel at the novelties for sale—a candle that looked exactly like a salami, a telephone that purred like a cat . . . An ad for suppositories, a bowl of singing fruit. A woman in a black leotard proclaiming her total commitment to yogurt. Frank talk about male enhancement drugs—the dangerous delight of erections lasting more than four hours. Talk show confessions in breaking voices, lubricated with tears. A laugh track cackling on and on against a blacked-out screen, could be a program error. An ad for a certain special brand of pen that could write a line four miles long, or an entire novel, take your pick; it came, apparently, to the same thing.

Often I muted the sound and simply let light and color wash over me. I remained wakeful in the deep dark hours, yielding to sleep only in the shallows before dawn.

Once, around midnight, I saw the strangest thing. The deaf were singing. Watching them with the sound off made it doubly eerie, as if for the moment I shared their deafness. The church—a bare-bones affair, no statues, no colored light, the pulpit, not the altar, in pride of place, everything plain, unmediated, designed for direct dealings—must have been Protestant.

I assumed that most of the people in the sanctuary had all-too-audible voices, but the camera kept circling and coming to rest on the first two pews where a special grouping of adults, a dozen maybe, were standing and beckoning, summoning unseen spirits, swaying to an unheard music. They looked to be sculpting—braiding the air—with their fingers, weaving nets and casting them—

   into an emptiness—

I don't know sign language; I'd always been intrigued by it. I'm pretty sure I caught the hand-sign for "believe," tapping the fore-finger of one hand to their brows, then dropping one hand, palm down, into the clasp of the other.

And doing my best to translate: touching the forehead . . . well, what else could it mean except "thought" . . . "thinking"?

But the clasped hands—did they signify "trust" or "a done deal"? Or (here came the cynic) "premature closure"?

Trying to keep my mind occupied in whatever way I could, I wasn't doing a very good job of it. I missed June—badly.

Twice, on the off-chance of casually running into her, I'd made my way down to the gourmet grocery on Fifty-Third where we'd first met. The place was crowded with strangers, all yuppie types, but no June.

Finally, after much to-ing and fro-ing, I decided to take a real risk. "Just happened to be in the neighborhood," I'd say. She'd have no time to shore up her defenses if I simply popped in without advance warning.

Five P.M., offices closing, the world going home for dinner.

What did I feel as I approached June's neighborhood? Nothing much—or something too mixed for naming. Coming close, I was of two minds about actually dropping in. I decided to let my legs decide.

"Hey! Just happened to be in the hood." We both laughed at my greeting; whenever I tried to sound contemporary, it came out as anything but. "Thought I'd stop by for a minute. How's it going?"

It had been over a month since she moved and it looked to me like she'd barely unpacked.

"I know, I know," she said, following my gaze. "Work's killing me. Can't find the time . . . What's up?"

She cleared a space for me on a couch cluttered with books and notes torn from a long legal pad, then settled herself in the director's chair opposite. Neither of us had the stomach for small talk, or for stirring up old issues. We sat, for a few painfully stretched moments, in silence to start. I noticed that one of my shoelaces was undone and stooped to tend to it.

"Absentminded or can't be bothered, as usual," she pounced.

"Tell me something I don't already know." I brought up the mounting pressures at work, a rumored budget squeeze, tangles with Medicaid, and (without naming names) more than my share of "difficult clients."

"So it's Michael again?"

"Among others."

"He's disappeared again?"

"Again." No way around the fact. "And with winter coming on —a hard winter if predictions are right."

72

June changed the subject abruptly after asking what my "plans" were for finding Michael and forcing me to admit that I had no plans—it wasn't my job to find him. I omitted mention of the stalking episode, an embarrassment even to think of.

Politeness reigned. She offered me something warming to drink, but I really had no intention of staying much longer. I didn't want to press my luck. I'd unburdened myself a little—June, for her part, not at all.

It was growing dark, inside and out; I didn't see how June could have failed to realize this. Time to turn on a table lamp, at least; time to kindle the hearth fires . . . Instead, we continued to sit on, making an effort at conversation as the shadows thickened around us—I, afraid of hastening my departure by mentioning lamps or darkness, and June, all too likely, signaling by this default how late it was and that it was high time for me to be on my way. Her face grew cloudlike, dim and insubstantial in the surrounding gloom.

Finally I made a motion to rise. "Only wanted to see how you've been getting along," I said.

"And now you see—"

This was even more awkward than I'd imagined, insofar as I'd imagined anything at all.

Still, I persisted. "I'd like to drop by again," I managed, "that be okay?" Then, to make sure there'd be no misunderstanding, I added, "Just to talk."

"Better give me a buzz first," she cautioned. "I might not be in. And, by the way, since you never bothered to ask, I'm seeing someone."

So soon? was on the tip of my tongue, but I thought the better of it and what escaped me was a barely audible "that's good . . . I guess . . ."

And, surely, I hadn't expected—anything. Standing in the foyer, summoning up the courage to press June's doorbell, my only thought had been, *What do I have to lose?* No expectations—but I couldn't help feeling disappointed, all the same.

11

Reception

I was the last person in the world who should have been entrusted with something like this, but chairing the office Social Committee fell out by lot. I hadn't been in charge of "planning the surprise" since the birthday party for Karina eight years ago, and my turn was long overdue.

The honoree was Don McNemeny so, however unwelcome, my task was relatively easy: not a birthday but a retirement, not a party but a "reception." No major fuss anticipated. The younger staffers had little reason to be aware of McNemeny's existence, tucked away as he was in the small room farthest from intake. The older social workers had been acquainted at some point, or had at least heard of him, but most of them had forgotten that he was with us, still among the living. His office was slap-up against the fire exit, and his specialty obscure—something to do with accounts, numbers, not people.

McNemeny's problem was that he lacked "people skills." Why he'd become a social worker was anyone's guess. (On the other hand, look who's wondering! I'd never been known for my social finesse; June wasn't the only one who'd noticed.)

In any case . . . whoever was in charge in the days of paper records had shunted him off to filing, then to crunching numbers. The few among us who knew he was still around had picked up rumors from time to time that McNemeny was a spy from Headquarters, a time-and-motion man from the Department of Social Welfare, sent to tattle on the rest of us. If that were true, he hadn't been very effective, our bad habits freely worsening through the years. Don McNemeny more than made up for the rest of the staff, though, showing up at the office half an hour before it opened, taking lunch at his desk, and nearly always the last to quit at closing time.

Since any disruption of those habits would take time getting used to, I thought it would be tactful to consult with McNemeny well before the reception, even to invite him in on the planning, if he were willing. I decided to present him with the news right away.

Have I mentioned that McNemeny was the quintessential nerd —OCD to perfection? (And, yes, I know, I'm hardly the one to comment.) With him, though, it was impossible to ignore. True to form, he wore a belt *plus* suspenders, plastic shirt pocket protector with pens clipped to it, lined up like military decorations. Next to him, I'm Mr. Normal, I thought with some relief, but maybe it was simply that McNemeny wore his difference on the outside, did nothing to hide it. He startled a little at my entrance but continued what he was doing, neatly divesting his sandwich of its wax paper wrap, then tossing the ends of his tie over his shoulder before digging in.

White bread, pale pink luncheon meat . . . everything to do with the man seemed colorless.

"Mind if I?"—I hesitated. He nodded but did nothing to help me as I cast about for a place to sit. I was struck by the absence of a client's chair. Desk, lamp, and at least two chairs counted as standard operating equipment in our outfit, the bare basics, yet his place was surprisingly cozy, snug in neglect. I spotted a stool for the computer over in the corner and wheeled it into position facing McNemeny.

Sensing my intrusiveness, I vowed to be brief.

"I've been assigned—" I began, settling myself. He turned on me an utterly blank look as I explained. "I figured you wouldn't want to be taken by surprise . . ."

He nodded. That much I'd gotten right.

Then I misspoke, uttered the p-word.

"Party? Must you?" he pleaded.

"A reception, then. You're not going to get out of more than thirty years of service without something!"

He sighed.

It would be, I promised, a simple gathering in the staff conference room. I didn't trouble to consult him on the cake. There had to be a cake, if only to make it worth their while for others to show up. The Social Committee had argued over the inscription. "So long, Sucker" was one suggestion, put forward with what seriousness I can't say. (Rumor had it that McNemeny had worked without a raise all these years.) In the end, we chose his name and dates of service, 1968–2000, in chocolate cursive on a vanilla background.

Tombstone and epitaph—I wasn't the only one to see it that way.

The designated hour arrived. We'd decorated the cake table with yellow crepe paper to brighten things up, arranged matching yellow napkins, paper plates, and yellow paper cups, and centered everything around a punch bowl with a sparkling red passion (non-alcoholic) fruit punch. Those few simple touches of color cheered up the room quite a bit.

We'd debated the gift and I turned out to be the only dissenter when they decided on a coffee-table book: a deluxe, leather-bound photo album. Maybe I was thinking of myself, of my own future—the album seemed so inappropriate, so useless, in a case like this. Did McNemeny even own a coffee table? I asked. Did anyone know? If, as seemed likely, McNemeny had neither visitors nor family, the album would remain empty. But how about *ancestors*? Everyone has parents and grandparents, the others insisted. The truth was, nobody wanted to spend a single minute more trying to dream up a gift for McNemeny. Outvoted and unable to come up with any suggestions for something really suitable, I had no choice but to agree on the album. *No point getting bent out of shape over this,* I told myself. And why should I care? Who was McNemeny to me?

The card accompanying the gift was standard and, again, wildly off the mark. Inscribed "The real YOU!!" (about which not one of us had an inkling) with a cartoon man lounging on the beach, tall drink nestled in the sand beside him, a bikini-clad figure strolling past, curlicue waves on the horizon, and a smiley-faced sun beaming over all of it. Inside, we'd added brief messages—the usual mishmash of funny and soppy: "The glow gets rosier . . . A joyful tomorrow . . . *Tempus fugit . . .*"

"If you don't come in Sunday, don't come in Monday" was signed "the Management," Karina's idea of humor. Two of the women from intake had written "We'll miss you"—the biggest stretch of all.

We'd tried to solicit testimonial letters from surviving retirees, people who might have known McNemeny better and might possibly have something personal to say, but people are so temporary, most of the names on the list turned out to be merely that—names. The two who responded praised McNemeny's patience, diligence, and modesty—nothing unexpected there; yet one mentioned his "wry humor" and "sage counsel" as well—news to us. Also "his erudition." Who knew of his graduate degree in jurisprudence from Columbia? He'd been too shy to litigate or teach, as I learned subsequently, and had somehow fallen into our outfit. Out of the frying pan into the fire, you'd think.

The ceremony opened with Karina striking a coffee spoon against the table in an attempt to bring us to order. It took longer than it should have, for the prospect of a free hour had brought with it a holiday mood.

It fell to me to introduce the proceedings. I can't remember what I finally came out with, only that I'd debated beforehand how to start things off. (*It's my pleasant duty to introduce . . . ? It's my sad duty . . . ? . . . my sad pleasure to . . . ?*) All I wanted to say was, *Everybody situated? Well, fine, then—I'm off . . .* And, in my desperation to get the business over with, I'm sure I spoke too rapidly for anything I said to make the slightest difference.

What I remember best is that right after the gift had been presented and the official words of praise spoken (with "reliability" brought up how many times?), one of the youngsters jumped to his feet, clamoring for McNemeny himself to speak.

I cringed, knowing it was a joke. I felt confident that McNemeny would refuse the invitation, though.

"Why, yes," he agreed, "I would." Last thing anyone expected.

Which goes to show how little anyone knows. McNemeny surprised us by positioning himself front and center, alongside the cake and the punchbowl. Then he paused—but only for an instant—fingering a trace of something white (medicinal?) at the corner of his lip, gave a little cough to ratchet up his voice, and began.

"I *would* like to say a few things"—as if the idea had been his. But I was all ears, as curious as the next person.

After a few words of thanks, he spoke of being free now to say "nothing but true things . . . unclamped from custom, at last . . ."

He started off with his memory of a mugging, how he'd tried to learn from it. He'd been strolling down Amsterdam Avenue early one Saturday morning. It was so early that there seemed to be no one up and about. He'd passed Columbia Law School and was heading north toward Teachers College when—out of nowhere—two teenagers confronted him, forced him up against a wall, demanding his wallet and his watch.

He'd refused, yelled at the top of his lungs, slipped free of his jacket, and broken loose. All for a wallet with less than thirty dollars in it. A wallet and a drugstore watch. What if he'd been stopped at gunpoint? What was a life worth, weighed against such trifles?

"You never know what you're going to do at a time like that . . ." was what he'd learned.

For a second, I thought McNemeny was going to give us a regular police spiel about being prepared for muggings, rehearsing your reaction and plan of action in advance, but it was nothing of the kind. He was in a plunge, deep and deeper, into the personal.

"You never know . . ." McNemeny shook his head. "I tell myself I'd hand over wallet and watch and everything I own in a heart-beat—that I'd rather be cheated, rather be the man who *bought* the Brooklyn Bridge than the one who sold it—but in the crunch, up against that wall, I can't promise . . . I still don't know. That mugging happened nearly thirty years ago, half a lifetime almost, and I'm still asking, 'What will I do when put to the test . . . ?'"

It started with small glances. Soon, the restlessness of those listening became palpable, people shifting noisily in their metal chairs. A stage yawn, hard to miss, from someone directly in front of me.

But McNemeny, on a roll now, seemed oblivious to any of this. Oblivious—or determined, in spite of it. With trembling fingers, he adjusted his bow tie and rambled on. It was as if he'd only now begun to breathe after decades of holding in.

There was a dream he wanted to share with us, some particular meaning he tried, but could not, get across. He started off on a light note, a joke, which only the few old-timers, laughing dutifully, seemed to recognize as such: "I was on the rumble seat . . . occupied," then, by some twist I failed to follow, he was on the Staten Island ferry, facing the great arc of the Verrazano Bridge. Then, another turn: the ferry became the Circle Line with this huge crowd of tourists on board. They were cruising Manhattan Island, the East River, smooth water, bridge after bridge, approaching the Triboro. But the bridges were burning, people pressing up against the rail to get a good look, and they were singing; he struggled to break free of the crowd, shouting, "I'm not a tourist—I *live* here!" but could hardly breathe, words in a whisper, he couldn't move for the pressure of "wall-to-wall people" at his back—"people singing and the bridges burning . . ."

Then, unaccountably (for it was only a dream), he was sobbing. Anyone's guess, the words still coming—a clatter—stick, stone—not a shimmer of sense. Call it a senior moment, a transient ischemia, all I know is I'd have picked up and left that very moment if I could. It was horribly embarrassing—for anyone, but especially for McNemeny—so out of character (the character we'd established) for him. Karina laughed outright—from nervousness or shock. Around me, others were whispering, "He's gone off the deep end" . . . "He's *lost* it . . ." everyone hoping he'd get a grip on himself, pull himself together. And I too couldn't help wishing the old nonentity back. Someone clapped, another joined in—like lighting a match; the applause, a flicker at first, caught, gathered, and spread. It was unforgivable: we refused to hear him out. We covered our embarrassment with beating hands.

And, no question: this time it registered. McNemeny broke off at once. He gave a hard swallow, words he would not say now, or ever. His mouth grew small, lip-seam tight, a hyphen; we'd muzzled him, all right. It was over. Although he didn't step away at once, for all intents and purposes he'd already left us, packed up, shut the lid, and snapped the locks. It could have been a stand-in, speaking a few faraway "thank-yous" in his stead.

There were no further surprises as the reception wound down. McNemeny had put on one of those smiles that say *don't ask, don't ask,* so I doubt that anyone did ask him what his retirement plans were. People fetched their allotted portions of cake and punch and carried them back to their desks. They pumped the honoree's hand on their way out, saying what people always say: "Back to the salt mines!" and "Keep in touch!"

And then McNemeny took his leave, back to his burrow. I was too ashamed to check up on him, but willing to bet that's where he went, and that he stayed on until the dot of five. Where else *could* he go?

More than one person intimated afterward that McNemeny must have been drunk to give the speech he did. Ergo: he *was* drunk. I couldn't accept this but said nothing to contradict it. Why do we think a man has to be drunk to speak what's on his mind?

Anyway, it took only a minute or two before McNemeny was back to himself (the man we'd recognize), the man who never made a ripple.

The whole business, from start to finish, left a sour taste in my mouth. Others must have felt the same—the Social Committee tidied up in silence. What remained of the cake was wrapped and shelved in the fridge for the next day's coffee break. McNemeny had indicated that he didn't want to take any "extras" home with him, not even the slice with his name on it, the piece I'd taken pains to keep intact for him. I forget what excuse he gave. I crumpled up the crepe paper tablecloth, now badly stained, and stashed the unused paper plates, napkins, and cups in the supply cabinet, on hand for future festivities. Except for Karina's, "He should have kept all that under his hat," and "It's the quiet ones you have to watch out for," no one said a word.

And after that? Back at my desk, it crossed my mind that McNemeny might have second thoughts about the cake—and wouldn't it be a nice gesture for me to bring him the slice with his name on it to wish him well again? There were no appointments holding me back. Staring at the same file folder until closing time, I got no work done, but, coward that I am, I never stirred from my chair. I told myself that I was respecting McNemeny's privacy by not interfering—that inaction, in this case, was the greater kindness. I almost (don't laugh!) made myself believe this, so intricate the twist of motive, so cunning, one can only marvel.

12

Realism

My usual nervous stomach.

The atmosphere before this month's staff meeting was predict-ably heavy—charged with portent. I expected a general browbeat-ing (with pointed, particular applications) and grew increasingly restless as the hour approached, unable to sit at my desk and take advantage of a morning free from appointments by catching up on paperwork, as I assumed everyone else was doing.

Instead, I wandered the intake area, scanning the posters on the walls, saying no to drugs, urging hope for HIV. I read the Serenity Prayer over Nova's desk, slowly, but with no discernible benefit. I paced, pausing to chat here and there, borrowing aspirins from Rosa, an antacid from Sue. Sue flinched when I passed her desk—I gathered she'd been busy e-mailing something personal on com-pany time.

The blacks among us were reasonably well integrated but there was not one without an empowerment poster: Martin Luther King, Muhammad Ali, James Brown, Shirley Chisholm, Langston Hughes. No Eldridge Cleaver, of course, and no rappers.

Jack's decorations had a different slant, a distinct personal im-print. He was new to the office and specialized in CAMIs and SAMIs—chemical abusers and substance abusers with mental illness. The MISAs and MICAs—mentally ill substance and chemical abusers went to others. (The difference between MISAs and SAMIs, MICAs and CAMIs? Different forms to be filled out and different funding—my best guess.) Jack put up with more bureaucratic nonsense than the rest of us; he didn't fight it, didn't try to explain it. I think he was grateful for *any* structure in his world, which gave me some idea how chaotic his life had been.

His bulletin board was crowded with addresses of methadone clinics and detox centers. A recovering alcoholic and one-time druggie himself, Jack was one of the agency's few certified success stories. Having "been there, done that," he had a kind of authority that commanded respect with all but the most hardened clients. There were no framed mottos over his desk, only a hand-printed job done in block letters:

I DRANK TO YOUR HEALTH AND LOST MY OWN

Aside from this message, there were few personal touches to be seen anywhere in the intake area or anywhere on the premises. Unlike most offices, there were no family photos—one of those security precautions I had no quarrel with. You never could tell how far a client, driven by hate, or love, might go.

Our meeting that day was billed as a "brown bag luncheon get-together," meaning send-outs to Subway or Wendy's or Cuban-Chinese from that hole-in-the-wall down the street, then on to business with popping-can and paper-rattling accompaniments.

Martin, who was "into meditation," brought his hands together and bowed to his veggie burger before unwrapping it. Karina had her high protein meal-deal in a bottle, so I knew she was dieting again and likely to be in a foul mood. We all had our little food foibles here in the so-called developed world.

Me—I'd brought from home my usual Swiss cheese on whole wheat with a dab of mustard. Apple and Twinkie for dessert. I had only one or two lunch variations during the week; it was too much bother even to have to *think* about what to eat.

"Get a load of this!" Jack, who was sitting next to me, gave a little hoot. He was taking a night course for extra credit. Exam on Friday, and he was using his spare minutes to bone up on the text-book. Every other paragraph seemed to be highlighted in yellow.

"Looks like you've found something interesting," I said.

"I'll say." And he was eager to talk about it. "Did you know that psychotherapy traces its roots back to the Inquisition?"

"The Inquisition? Really? Well, if so," I drew the obvious con-clusion, "that should chasten us some." The connection struck me as pretty far-fetched at first, but less so as he went on. Similar busi-ness, really, the more I thought about it: the face-to-face encoun-ter, the probing of motive, the peeling away of disguise . . .

Our conversation came to an abrupt halt when Karina, using an unopened can of Diet Coke, gaveled us down to the business at hand.

What can I say about what followed? The theme? The drift?

Flexibility and strictness. "This is what we have to work with." The Serenity Prayer, as usual, but only the first three verses asking for grace and courage to accept what cannot be changed, to change what could be changed, and the wisdom to distinguish one from the other. Nobody I knew quoted the full text, invoking, as it did, hardship now with happiness in the life to come.

But back to the gist of the meeting . . . Sympathy and skepticism, the subdued crunching of teeth, the nervous scratching of a pen. "Realism" was the watchword. Could Karina spell out what she meant by "realism"? She could, she did. Double-checking need and unreported income. More oversight of the intake process and more stringent questioning of the necessity for particular services. The word "fraud" mentioned twice. She went on. Mounting backlogs . . . Face-to-face time with clients was to be kept to the minimum. How often the hard decision was best. Limits (I was particularly touchy here) had to be set on how many times a client could miss an appointment before he was let go.

It was that old song: Our job was to build confidence, motivat-ing clients to solve their own problems. The magic words "self-determination." A cautionary tale trotted out once again for the edification of newcomers. How many times had I heard this story about a nameless, well-intentioned, but novice, social worker who wants so much for her client to succeed at his first job that she starts giving him wake-up calls at quarter to seven every morning?

Then the client disconnects his phone.

Then the client quits his job, disappears.

Then the social worker quits her job.

Sometime after that, the case goes to the Dead File.

QED, prompting a slew of favorite slogans: "The client is not well served" . . . "We're not here to run other people's lives" . . . And so on, and so forth.

Karina was only three or four years my senior. Fake blonde (black roots). Still attractive, I supposed, although I'd never been attracted to her. She had this overbite; when she leaned forward for emphasis, her large breasts bunched up—I couldn't help noticing these things. I wish I didn't.

She went on with it, ever "stricter" and "more stringent." More stringent monitoring of services to make sure the therapeutic plan was coherent and up to date. Stricter attention to confidentiality. No personal agendas. No "radical or untested" approaches. Individual discretion, a luxury from the past, would be less and less affordable going forward. A warning about acting outside the "number of the law"—whatever "number" might mean in this context. (How about the *spirit* of the law?) Did she actually mean the listing number in the statute book? Was this a masked allusion to some recent incident? If so, the scuttlebutt had not yet reached my desk.

"Often, the most we can ask of our clients is a return to baseline. We shouldn't expect breakthroughs." (Was Karina staring at me as she said this?) "In a perfect world . . ." she continued. Her hands lifted, fluttered, fell.

Obviously, this wasn't a perfect world. What we faced was a lowered budget ceiling. What we had to focus on were reimbursements—billable hours and milking every penny to which we were entitled from Medicaid. Looking a little farther down the road, it would be either heavier caseloads or layoffs we'd be facing.

"That's the deal," she wrapped it up, "take your choice . . ."

By the time Karina opened the floor to questions, all you could hear was the *peck-peck-peck* of the big clock overhead. When one person, then another, finally summoned up the nerve to speak, there were more statements than questions. The gist of it was no one wanted layoffs. It was no choice at all.

13

Eye in the Slot

Another month passed. I awaited word from or about Michael. None came.

Half an hour before the next staff meeting, Karina called me aside.

"Got a minute?" she asked. I took this as a summons not a question, and followed meekly into her office. She was wearing fancy shoes, I noticed, with pointed toes, and breakneck heels that gave her a good inch or two on me. "Would you get that?" She gestured at the open door. *Now what?* There would be no invitation to sit down since Karina herself remained standing. "You seem . . ." her fingers cashiered stray threads from the lining of her sleeve, "distracted."

"I don't mean to pry," she added.

I asked her to please not beat around the bush.

"Well, okay, then. About Gary."

I should have known, *I should have known*. Gary had been on my watch for more than a year. That business, a couple sessions before, about sitting at lunch across from a nodding friend and worrying that his friend's head was about to fall off should have been a red flag to me.

"What happened?"

"Damnfool nothing, at first . . ." Apparently he'd been stopped from trying to enter the building while toting a gun in a paper bag. The paper bag was to fool the metal detector, although the gun was only a water pistol—and plastic. "Whoever was at the door— Arnie, I think—gave him a good talking-to and let him go. Can you imagine?"

"But if he was only bluffing—?"

"Only! To start, maybe . . ." Turned out, there'd been another incident on a bus the next day. No toy—a real gun this time, and he'd gotten his hands on some ammo. He'd been swiftly apprehended. The charge this time was threatened aggravated assault.

"By the way . . . your last meeting with him was when?"

Two weeks . . . or three . . . ? I'd have to check my calendar. I didn't mention Gary's fantasy of heads rolling, not that I was hiding anything; Karina would come to it in due course if she checked my monthly records.

Right then the phone rang and she pounced upon it.

"Uh-huh," she said, and, "No . . . I didn't know . . ." and, "Oh, hell . . ." waving me out.

I tried to settle back at my desk but, finding it impossible to concentrate, wandered off to the coffee-maker where a small group had foregathered. The mood was gloomy and the usual cynicism prevailed. "Keep your ass covered and your head above water," that sort of thing. We'd caught wind of the impending budget crisis weeks before, but funding was normally tight around here, so we tried to make light of it, saying, "It's always something" and "So what else is new?" We expected a rerun of the previous meeting.

We were mistaken. Karina had brought along her supervisor this time, a time-and-motion man from the City Department of Social Welfare and, despite their urging to "interrupt us anytime with your questions," we sat through most of their performance in silence. *Her* performance, I'm tempted to say, but the two were closely orchestrated.

I was tuning in and out, my attention drawn to Jack's discarded Styrofoam cup with its jagged, bitten-down rim, as if to a speaking thing.

This time, they were calling for more than the anticipated belt-tightening. The caseload increases coming our way would be drastic, meaning less time allocated to individual clients, more emphasis on crisis management.

"No one expects you to work miracles," Karina stressed. The main thing was to avoid emotional exhaustion and burnout—what she called "compassion fatigue."

"Even metals fatigue," her supervisor added.

Something else I found ominous: a passing remark about how little cost-effective were any efforts to change those "homeless by choice."

Michael's case was all too likely to be dubbed exactly that. But he wasn't costing us a penny at the moment. I knew that his room at St. Joe's had been reassigned. Beyond this, I'd heard nothing, not one word to prove that he'd ever darkened my threshold.

My sleep, when it came, was porous. A small cough could bring me to my feet.

From the other side of my too-thin bedroom wall, I heard panting and grappling, a dark stifled moan. I thought of animals coupling, of low, distant forms of life. I could hear the least scratch of sound, the rustle of water from the apartment above me as it started through the pipes, voices coming through the faucet, the words barely intelligible, moving through a constant stream of sighs.

One night, I was startled awake in the small hours by the creaking of elevator cables and the muffled footfall of somebody stepping off at my floor. I waited for the clinking of keys, the sound of a door opening and shutting—but what I heard was a soft, ghostly padding, dog or cat perhaps, pacing up and down the hallway.

Something moving on buttered paws . . .

Then—a jingling. Could have been keys, coins, anything.

I roused myself, tiptoed to the door, raised the metal lid, and pressed my eye to the slot, but there was nothing to be seen but the facing wall. I checked my two locks and my chain-bolt. *Everything fast.*

Again, I stared through the narrow aperture: The shock! An eye came back at me.

Eye would not budge from eye.

It might have been a neighbor, there was no way for me to tell, I didn't know my neighbors, chose not to put my name on the apartment door—few people did.

Although I knew the slot worked as a one-way window, I ducked down to make absolutely certain I was out of view. Crouched there, behind my triple locks.

He might have been one of those jokers who'd been stealing doormats from the building; I recalled reading about it in a notice posted in the lobby. Not from my floor, but from two, three, and seven. A stunt like that suggested pranksters on the loose, more mischievous than truly harmful. Real thieves would have no use for doormats.

I couldn't tell whether the man waiting on the other side of the door was still there. (I assumed it was a man—unlikely that a woman would be wandering alone at that time of night.) When I heard nothing further, I started to wonder whether I'd been dreaming, or even whether the apparition might have been a reflection of my own eye—reflexivity gone amuck!

But then—when I was about to turn and go back to bed—my bell rang. Someone really *was* out there. Again the bell rang. And again. The joke, if joke it was, had gone too far. I opened the slot once more, and this time he must have been standing farther back: I could make out the bridge of a nose, and a mouth—moving. The voice was faint:

"It's me," he said. As if I'd know. "Can we talk a minute?"

Carefully, trying to make no sound, I lowered the lid while he talked on.

He'd lost his key, he explained, and couldn't remember anything, not his apartment number, his name, not even his floor—all the floors looked the same.

It would be nice to say that I invited him in, that I lived in such a world. Or even that I stepped out into the hallway to see if I could be of some use. Or simply encouraged him to talk on, keeping the door as buffer between us. Or said something—anything— a word to let him know there was someone else alive and listening. But I did none of those things. All I could think of was calling the police, or at least the super. The fact is, you can't tell whom to trust these days and, like I said, I didn't know my neighbors. Didn't and don't.

Resting my hand on the door knob, thinking to steady it, I felt my fingers web together—seemed like I couldn't separate them if I tried. That was scary, too.

That man could have been anyone, thief, strangler, arsonist, or simply an Alzheimer's patient put out on the ice by his children.

I waited for him to tire and give up, but he lingered; and I continued pretending not to be there, my fingers locked on the knob to keep it from turning.

It seemed ages before he moved on.

Christmas came and went. For New Year's Eve, I'd made a resolution to turn in early, and I would have kept it if not for the neighbors. I'd tramped over four miles in the snow. Clean, bright motes, flecks of gladness, filled the air. That afternoon, I'd taken in a light-hearted (forgettable) movie, and by the time I arrived home I had trouble remembering not only the story but even what it was called. On my way back, I'd stopped to take in the spectacle of firefighters gathered round their idling truck, pelting each other with snowballs. They were grown men—big men, made huge by their winter padding—yelping like schoolboys, tumbling to the ground in mock death throes. The snow was subsiding by then, but there was already a four- or five-inch cover underfoot.

With my feet sodden, toes and fingers numb, I was grateful to be back inside. *The right kind of tiredness*, I told myself, expecting to sleep the night through. I felt pretty virtuous then, planning to wake early, refreshed, eager not to waste the first day of the year. But the sound of doors opening and shutting in the hallway, elevator bells, the salvos of party horns, music and voices leaking out, made sleep impossible. So I switched on the television and, like a million others, watched the glitter-ball drop in Times Square. If only that would have ended it . . . But—dream on!—in the apartment above me the partying grew ever more frantic. Bongos banging; people in iron clogs dancing with heavy machinery, what it sounded like.

Back to bed only to toss and turn. I tried to read but—*no use!*—stalled on the first page. Tried a mix of white wine and Tension Tamer tea, but the tension did not abate. To pass the time, I startled doodling on a piece of paper towel. Its surface was coarse, so the ink bled in surprising ways. A face of stains emerged . . . *strange* . . . an eye in a shallow cup, a thick blot for the trench between nose and lip. It was nobody's face in particular. Might have been me watching myself, or anyone, simply a watcher. It might have been Michael.

Say it was: I started to talk to that paper face as though it were Michael in person: "What are you keeping from me? I am sick of secrets. Tell me . . . you trusted in Dumpster food because you believed—what? Because you believed it was put there by someone you trusted. Like June said: 'a connection' . . .

"Tell me who with—"

14

Shackled

Gary's case was in court. By shifting a couple of appointments and making a giant pretzel from a pushcart do for lunch, I was able to be there. I hardly recognized Gary with his hair shorn and dressed as he was in dark suit and tie. He must have been heavily tranquilized—I saw none of his signature head-fastening gestures. Whether he was paying attention to the proceedings was anyone's guess.

Two days later, I left the morning session to check in at the office and made it back by early afternoon, arriving as the guilty verdict was being pronounced. Gary was immediately handed over into "protective custody," and escorted offstage for a wardrobe change. I was present for the sentencing, and that heart-sinking moment—a moment is all it takes—for a free man to walk out the door and a look-alike puppet to shuffle back in his place. Gary-the-prisoner was wearing one of those bright orange jumpsuits; he must have put up some resistance for his ankles were shackled, and his handcuffs latched to a chain around his waist (a "transport belt," I think they call it). I made an attempt at a wave, my hand at half-mast; he glanced briefly back at me: eyes and mouth, bare oblongs, vacant. Then a glimmer, a momentary parting of clouds, a glint, the twist of a smile or grimace in recognition, and he turned to face the judge. The trial was about to be wrapped up.

One of the bailiffs carried his civilian clothes. Casting about the nearly deserted courtroom for a familiar face, he lighted on mine. As soon as Gary had been hustled off for booking, shouting over his shoulder, "Give my regards to the free world!" the officer headed my way, Gary's suit and tie draped over his arm. I backed off a step or two at his approach, protesting, "I had nothing to do with—" but the bailiff wasn't buying that. "The prisoner says you did," he said, handing the clothes over for me to deal with. A rented costume, as I'd suspected; the outfit had to be paid for. The tie must have been borrowed. From someone. Who failed to show. I took the thing back to my office and folded it into one of the less cluttered drawers in my desk.

The jury had deliberated for less than an hour; the judge gave Gary two years. Parole possible in—I've already forgotten, for, as it turned out, they needn't have bothered.

The phone woke me early the next morning. Quarter of seven, to be exact. I didn't welcome it. With the kind of nights I'd been having, a little predawn slumber was sometimes all I could count on.

It took me longer than it should have to recognize Father Evans's voice. I'd forgotten that I'd ever given him my home number.

"Look, I've got a bit of news." He hesitated before going on. "I thought it might be important. I'm not absolutely certain, but . . . You be the judge."

Cleaning out the storage room, he'd found a letter. "More a note, I guess you'd say . . . It could be from anyone. But, for some reason, it makes me think of Michael."

"Why's that?" I pressed. "And I'd really be interested in knowing who it's to—"

"Hear me out," he said, then dithered, "But it's printed, so, sure, it could be from anyone . . ."

Without a salutation or address, all he could do was to speculate that the note was meant for someone with whom he—whoever wrote it—kept in fairly constant communication.

"It's a hunch," he emphasized, "only a hunch."

"Okay, but you haven't said—what makes you think it's Michael?"

"There's something . . ." he answered with maddening vagueness. "Look, I can't prove it, but hear me out . . ."

It didn't seem to be much, at first.

" '. . . The blue sweater you left is nice. Only a little big in the arms and neck hole.' . . . I grant you this could be anyone, so why do I think it's Michael? It's what comes next—about food. Are you listening?"

"I'm all ears." I meant it.

"So okay . . . 'I love the special dessert. Dark chocolate you know how I like it. Not the milky. I write in the notebook you gave me every day. Do you feel the breeze when I pass? When I think of you?' "

I, too, thought this had to be Michael, how Michael would sound if ever he allowed himself to confide in anyone. Really, though, I had no evidence, no basis for deciding one way or the other.

But then—it seemed relevant—I recalled an afternoon of steady downpour when he came in drenched to the skin and so chilled that his teeth were chattering. All I could do was offer him a roll of paper towels and invite him to drape his jacket over a stool, which I moved close to the radiator. For most of our session, Michael remained standing next to the chair in front of the radiator—getting warm, of course, but also guarding the jacket. When, color and warmth restored, he finally sat down in the client's chair opposite my desk, his eyes never left the thing. As if he were afraid it might magically disappear (as magically as it had materialized for him?). Or could be, it occurred to me, that he thought of the jacket, too, as a gift from someone, someone terribly important to him.

What sort of jacket? Ordinary, worn, moldy. Army surplus, I'm pretty sure—made of heavy-duty canvas, and full of pockets—perfect for scavenging. But it was also too small and must have felt stiff as armor after the radiator, the way he struggled to put it back on.

Needing to clear my head, I walked to work.

On the safety island between the uptown and downtown lanes in the middle of Seventy-Sixth and Broadway, an old woman sat feeding a hungry horde of municipal pigeons. She looked pretty disheveled and possibly hungry herself—homeless maybe, or maybe not—there were no bundles of stash to give her away; all she had was the broken loaf in her lap.

There must have been fifty birds, a regular traffic jam, poking and jabbering, crowding the old woman's feet.

Suddenly she turned a rheumy eye upon me.

"I'm feeding my family," she said.

There was nothing I could do but stand there, avoiding eye contact by staring at my shoes, waiting for the light to change.

"They're my family," she repeated, in case I'd not heard the first time, "I'm feeding them."

And all morning long the word "family" seemed to be lodged in my ear; I could hear nothing else properly.

That night, a strange thing happened. Normally, I fight sleep; when I do succumb it's to plunge deeply. This time, I seemed to float in some liminal space instead, a space neither shallow nor deep, where I dreamed yet knew I was dreaming . . .

. . . Out on the fire escape, I'm not wearing shoes, but my feet don't feel a thing. Stepping lightly to start, laddering upward, I'm pointed, aimed at—directed. *Where?* (It isn't a question in the dream, there are no questions within the dream—unless the dream itself . . . ?)

Rung after rung, ever faster I go, tracking—*what?* (The dream does not specify.) Up and up, and then—

> nothing
>> spacious nothing—

The rungs break off in empty air.

A blink and I step off sideways and I'm—not falling but swimming, loosening like laughter *how easy this is how easy* and I—

15

Leap

I was awake then, totally awake.

Trying not to think of the clock, hoping to sleep again, proved fruitless. The digital whirred and emitted hours, minutes, seconds, fractions of seconds, in pulsing lights.

Three A.M. My teeth chattered. Something rustling outside . . . The downpour, when it came, came in gusts, so loud and busy that it sounded like applause.

I padded over to the window, tabbed the shade, and peered out. The street rippled and shone. Only a few cars were moving. A taxi flashing its hazards was double-parked at the intersection, its driver slumped over the steering wheel.

A lone figure, featureless in shadow, emerged from a darkened doorway, staggered past the cab and on down the street.

I thought of Michael, recalled the note Father Evans had found. *I write in the notebook you gave me every day . . .*

At that moment it seemed clear to me—it could not be clearer—that the note was from Michael and to whom it was written. As if I'd been climbing a ladder of inference, dutiful step after step, only to find there was no top rung, and—forced to back down or to continue—chose to continue, stepping off onto nothing but air.

I say "chose" to continue, but there was no pause for deliberation, no hesitation, it was all shockingly effortless.

Then again, mulling it over, I thought I could name that leap, the step that wasn't there. "It wasn't her doing," he'd blurted out after his bout with rat-poisoned food. *Her* doing . . . ? How many women were there in his life? None reported; one, by biologic necessity. So, say the note was written to his mother . . . That he believed she was leaving food for him as she moved through the city . . . It wasn't that far-fetched: Dumpster . . . feeding . . . would be the associative links, steps, rungs, call them what you will. But here I'd have to assume, as I hadn't before, that Michael knew something about his Dumpster birth.

Arriving at the office early, I jotted down on the back of an office memorandum all I could recall from my ladder dream. I stashed the page out of sight in my bottom desk drawer next to Gary's tie. After I'd sobered up on a couple cups of coffee and worked through my morning's docket, I took down my DSM manual and riffled through its pages. My hope was to find a label, a tag, something that sounded official, helping to place Michael's case at a cool distance and discourage any further "leaps" on my part.

The manual was chock-full of memorable delusions. There was the case of a husband jealous of his wife's many imaginary lovers, believing that the headlights of passing cars were signaling amorous messages to his wife in a code she'd concocted for this purpose . . . And my favorites: A woman afraid to leave her apartment because the sound that she (but no one else) could hear was ultrasound beamed at her nonexistent fetus . . . A man convinced he had two noses and that people avoided mentioning it through politeness, choosing to avert their eyes instead . . . In all these instances, the diagnosis of delusion, highlighted by quirkiness and extravagance, was obvious.

With Michael, no such markers. And yet, it seemed clear to me then that he suffered from delusion—unshared, uncorroborated belief, belief backed up by nothing but sheer insistence.

But—*whose* insistence? Michael had not confided one word to anyone. My reading of his behavior was a hunch, a grappling in the dark, mere supposition.

And yet, and yet—what other explanation could there be?

It made perfect sense.

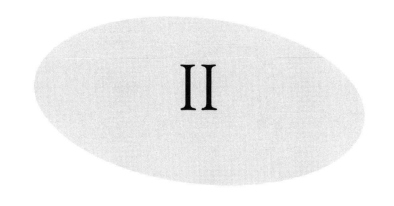

II

16

Weeping Statues, Etc.

Do something unexpected this week! was Nan's repeated advice, and my excuse for ducking into Our Lady of Consolation, a church I'd passed now and then on my walks. I'd never thought of taking a peek inside before; it was hardly what Nan had in mind, but I had reason to be curious and, without question, it would be doing something different.

For the past few days I'd been following a story on the radio about this particular church slated for demolition due to the changing demographics of the neighborhood.

There was a small crowd gathered at the door of one of the side chapels. I surprised myself by heading for it and lining up. I followed the procession of bowed heads, joined palms, and softly shuffling feet, of people moving like sleepwalkers, like shadows. It had been overcast all afternoon and the entryway seemed to be in deep twilight. Ahead, in the sanctuary, there were lights.

Curiosity drew me. Reports were that right after the closing was announced, a "miracle" had occurred: the statue of the Blessed Virgin in the sanctuary had begun to weep. The resident pastor Father Jim McBride, kissing the feet of the statue, had been shocked to find that the moisture tasted like human tears, the same faintly saline trace. The so-called tears had yet to be scientifically analyzed, but few of the faithful were waiting on tests. Even before the media took notice, news had traveled by word of mouth, and attendance at Mass had swelled beyond seating capacity. And there'd been "locutions," a word unfamiliar to me, though I suspected I'd dealt with these under a different name and nomenclature—visions and revelations and frequent reports of the sweet smell of sanctity surrounding the statue, the fragrance of roses, with no roses, no flowers of any kind, present.

In the midst of all the excitement, the local bishop, cited at length in the news account, had come through as a paragon of calm and common sense. "God can work in supernatural ways, but His ordinary grace at work in our day-to-day experience trumps the extraordinary every time." He'd quoted Scripture to his purpose: "Blessed are those who have not seen, yet believed."

And there I was. Expecting no blessing, I'd come to see.

As darkness gains density and presence, it's a fact, the primitive senses take over. I was not a little spooked. Around me, beads ticked. Candles wept. The sourness of damp wool and sweat filled my nostrils, the fatness of wax, laced with ghost-traces of incense— still sharp, faintly stinging.

Dry-eyed, unmoved, I felt all too obviously the stranger in their midst. "Stranger" is putting it mildly—"flaming heretic" would be more like it. There I was, wrapped in the surround-sound, the gentle hum of prayer, and I had no idea how to pray, how even to begin, how to address a prayer—to whom? *To Whom It May Concern?* But it did not concern, I remained convinced of that much. Privately, I pictured God, if I pictured anything at all answering to that name, as a sort of cosmic gas, infinitely expansive, utterly indifferent, a gas with lights in it—lights that took eons to reach us. Black holes; and the light always too late . . .

A tap on my shoulder. I flinched, shrank from the contact (imagining that someone had overheard my thoughts?), but it was simply an elderly gent trying to be helpful, pointing "right ahead!"— assuming I wouldn't want to miss the font coming up on my left. I did my best to slink by, hoping to pass unnoticed as I refrained from dabbling my fingers in holy water and blessing myself, unwilling to dip down on one knee when we entered the sanctuary and confronted the burnished silver box where the magic wafers were stored, steadfast in my refusal to make any gesture of recognition to an unreal world. I can't say it wasn't a strain, all the watchfulness required to steer my way past snares arranged so cunningly. Inhaling, exhaling, my breath seemed loud, almost as loud as the drone of "pray for us . . ." The line moved steadily, but oh so slowly, forward.

A printed card was slipped into my hand. The light was poor, the script old-fashioned cursive, curling, faint; I struggled to make out the words by mouthing them silently to myself: *Lord by thy . . . by thy what? . . . sweet and . . . ? . . . sweet and saving Sign . . .* The rest came easier: *Defend us from our foes and thine.*

Thou shalt open
And my mouth
O God make speed
O Lord make haste
Glory be to
As it was in

The heat must have been on full blast. Although I'd removed my overcoat and draped it over one arm, I felt no relief. And maybe the heat was the culprit in what followed: a white-haired woman, approaching the statue, fainted, but was snatched up in the nick of time by a couple standing nearby. They were stretching her out on a pew, a young woman was already dialing 911 on her cell phone, when the old woman bolted upright and—others making way for her—started with quick, uneven steps to resume her place in line.

Here, I suspected, before my very eyes, was a legend in the making, a tale of miraculous revival; it would exfoliate and bloom in afterlife as such stories do, adding to the lore of the weeping statue. I'd been a witness.

There'd been a spate of miracles reported recently, no locale too unlikely. Staring at the noonday sun in West Texas, a pious few had been granted a glimpse of the Blessed Virgin, dancing in the bright beams. She'd reappeared three times to record-breaking crowds, and she'd left messages. Some of the witnesses were reported to be suffering permanent retinal damage.

Inching closer . . .

"See her cheeks?" the woman ahead of me pointed. Something glinting like mica there. Tears? Who could say? What were tears, anyway? Nothing much: water, sodium chloride, mucin, a pinch of potassium or phosphate of something or other, a tinge of . . . I forget. But the face of the woman beholding the statue was glistening and, despite everything, I envied her tears—those living drops my grandmother called "the gift of tears" yet could not give to me. True, living tears: soul melt, the blood of spirit . . . My eyes were dry, always. With my tear ducts clogged from as far back as I can remember, I'd never known that outflow, that release. Instead, I remained high and dry on the parched sands of reason. Often I'd wake to the day with my eyes clamped shut. I wept through my nose—if that counted as weeping.

Dry eyes, dry soul . . . I had a client once who'd tattooed himself with a tear at the corner of one eye. Trying to wear his inside on the outside, I wondered . . . Or—just the opposite—desperate to dress himself in what he could not feel?

The statue seemed to be made of some contemporary ceramic or fiberglass material; I imagined it would feel smooth, cool to the touch. I didn't think I'd get up the nerve to touch it, though. There was a towel under the base. I remember reading that the pastor had moved the statue away from its usual standing place; it had been generating too much moisture, and the original site was close to an electrical outlet.

The line continued to inch forward. Ready or not, I was next. I studied the woman ahead of me as she unfolded her handkerchief and passed it lightly over the toes of the statue, pressed the cloth to her lips, then knelt and blessed herself.

My turn.

From up close, the Mother of God appeared to be faintly smiling—at *me*! So it was her smile, not her tears, that struck me first. The longer I stared, the more definite my impression became. Then

I noticed that she was also winking. Yes, winking! I had to stare down at my shoes to break the spell.

When I glanced up again, her face was smooth and impassive. But streaked with what did indeed look to be tears. I tracked the thread of wetness carefully: both eyes, one nostril, lower lip. There was a drop under her chin and a tiny puddle cupped in the hollow where throat met collar bone. Her sandaled feet, the folds of her robe, glistened, exuding some kind of moisture—sweat, maybe . . . Anyway, I was sweating. I ventured to put out my hand, to touch one foot and the hem of her garment, not daring to reach up and touch her face, although I longed to—as if that would put the question of what kind of moisture to rest. The dampness in the fold of her robe felt ever so slightly oily and the porcelain or fiberglass, or whatever the statue was made of, was surprisingly warm to the touch—why? Could the repeated massaging of hands have raised the temperature to that point? Or, maybe, the thought occurred to me, there might be some hidden heat source near the statue. (But, no, there was no electrical outlet nearby, I'd read that.) Still—the statue might have been hollowed out. Greased and warmed to suggest weeping. Something battery-operated, or maybe even a candle inside?

A phrase came to mind: *long ago, when wishes were of use . . .* The drone of the rosary continued:

". . . fruit of thy womb, Jesus . . ."

"I'll pray for you," the woman at my back whispered to the back of my neck.

Was I that obvious? I knew I had no right to be there among the believers. All the same, I took my time, staring at the statue. Too smooth, too sentimental to qualify as a work of art: the girl's unlined face seemed innocent of thought or care. One knee nudged forward, slightly bent, to relieve the monotony of her stance, I suppose; she wasn't going anyplace. Her hands were open, fingers wide apart, her arms impossibly elongated, gesturing, but however far they stretched, strengthless to gather, gather in—

We filed out through a back door where a small crowd of demonstrators had assembled. They carried homemade placards: A

MIRACLE—OUR LADY WEEPS and HEAR OUR PRAYER and, quaintly, URGENT, PLEASE! One of the larger ones proclaimed, F-A-I-T-H—FORSAKE ALL IN TRUSTING HIM. I was struck by the pallor of the sign-bearers, their drabness, how lumpy and unstylish their coats. Members of a television news crew were scurrying among them, trying to get the best angle on the scene, which must have been nothing more than a piece of street theater to them. I tried to duck when one of the cameras started to close in on me, of all people. A microphone on a long boom grazed my shoulder.

"What do you think?" A reporter in my face. I took a step backward and the camera followed. "I'm not a member here," I protested.

"Why'd you come, then?"

"Just curious," I said.

"Well, but you've seen her, you know what you've seen. What do you think?"

"Eyewash!" I thought this would do the trick. "A fairy tale. Here be dragons . . ."

But I was the only dragon present.

It was then that I happened to notice the mural on the wall of a building facing us across the street—of a dark lady in a blue mantle studded with gray (meant to be silver) stars, a spiky halo in orange (meant to be gold). She stood on a half shell of some sort, angry serpents writhing under her feet. The image was standard, vaguely familiar, I'd seen it before. Big with Latinos . . . The Virgin of Guadalupe, yes. Yet something about this particular mural seemed wrong. Crudely painted but, more than that, it was the expression on the lady's face. Something askew. One eye out of alignment did it, gave her a sly, niggling look. Did no one else notice?

Already the reporter had turned away from me in search of more promising material. Others must have been listening in. I could have dropped down on all fours with room to spare, the way the sign-bearers broke formation and the crowd parted to let me pass.

Why had I come? Not to mock, really not, but, clearly, I hadn't come there to pray. Had I secretly been hoping to run into Michael in a setting like this? Not likely. Michael was not a churchgoer. Delusional, faith-filled, maybe, but not a churchgoer. His non-affiliation was a matter of record in the accounts of the various Catholic and Protestant charities sponsoring him in the past.

So, why? Why had I troubled to travel the distance, only to make myself uncomfortable? What was I doing among these poor drabs who thought to storm heaven with cardboard placards and psalms? What was their argument? Simply: *need,* the argument from desire—desire surfeited by its own hunger? The logic was circular, the leap of faith: a loop.

What world did these people live in?

Not mine, to be sure. But, then again—I had no story to go by, and theirs was at least a storied world, thick with intimations and wonders.

A world alive with expectation—and delusion . . . And I couldn't help wondering what these people would do when the building closed (as I somehow knew it would) despite their prayers. What would it take, how much evidence to the contrary, how many disappointments would they have to experience before they relinquished their "miracle"?

One must face facts!

It started to drizzle. Halfway home, the rain began to beat down in earnest. I had no umbrella but decided to walk the rest of the way; already drenched, I could get no wetter. The cold and the open air seemed to clear my head.

I knew I'd behaved badly. I'd like to say it troubled me more.

Here and there were dark smudges against the walls; even on a night like this, the homeless were everywhere. A glint of eyewhite or shimmer of movement would give the person away. A lucky few had found refuge in the entryways to shops, but most of them, mere heaps and bundles to the casual eye, lay out on the sidewalk, flayed by the now-pelting rain.

I trudged on, cheered to find one man with enterprise who'd managed to rig up a tent with a broken umbrella and a tarpaulin and was completely hidden (and dry, I hoped) inside it. The only evidence of occupation was a DO NOT DISTURB sign in trickling letters, positioned like a doormat, plastered to the pavement in front.

Rummaging around the office library after work, I stumbled on some interesting items suggesting that delusions were not necessarily incorrigible.

Case in point: The text dubbed him "the Scriptmaster"—a man who believed he could cause things to happen simply by thinking them. An enterprising researcher made a video recording of an unfamiliar television program, playing it for the subject, pausing at strategic points in the unfolding drama to ask what would happen next. The subject confessed that he didn't know, and this admission marked the beginning of the end—end of delusion and the beginning of therapeutic progress.

It could be done. Delusions could be modified. Or—I cautioned myself not to go overboard—some could, some couldn't. The trick was to find out which beliefs were which. I was still obsessing over Michael, obviously, how I'd proceed, when and if—

17

Palimpsest

Walking was my only recreation. I walked myself into a trance sometimes. Afterward, sleep came more easily.

Late Saturday afternoon, despite a stiff breeze blowing, I was at it again. A strange cloud formation kept me company. Though tall buildings often blocked my view, I kept my eye out, trained on the sky as clouds bubbled over and diffused. The changes were dizzying, seamless . . . milky mountain . . . into tumbling bear with cubs . . . hats in a heap . . . in a spill . . . into wind-torn tree in tatters . . . spindrift . . . mist . . . until all that the eye could see seemed to be drowned in milk.

Then I stumbled on a little, low-growing, curly weed that had the audacity to raise its head, to live and flourish in a pavement crack, between blocks of bare concrete, where no living thing was ever meant to breathe, and it nearly brought me to my knees. I was wide awake, but light-headed—I'd skipped lunch.

Once more I found myself back at Our Lady of Consolation. There'd been no follow-up in the news, and there was nothing much to observe on-site. The protestors, apparently, had long since dispersed. The doors to the church were boarded up, with no notice posted, no way of telling whether demolition or renovation would soon be in the works.

Definite changes were underway across the street, though. The Guadalupe mural on the wall of the facing building had been painted over, first with a layer of white, then an impasto of the same blue, if I recall rightly, as the Virgin's mantle underneath. Someone must have complained about that painting; I guess I wasn't the only one who'd found it disturbing.

An odd thing: It seemed to me I could still see the eye of the Virgin, the one out of alignment with the rest of the face, lurking underneath, peering faintly through the overlay. Then again, after all my cloud-gazing, how could I be sure?

Curiosity drew me back twice after that. Both times, the skies were clear, no question of visibility. Still, nothing happening on the church building or grounds—or, at least, nothing observable from the outside; but the mural across the street was completely transformed. It looked now like an ad for Pepsi, something bubbly, anyway: a swinging teenage beach scene set against blue sea and sky. The lead female was leaping to catch a beach ball, her head thrown back in a frenzy of fun, curved lips glistening with laughter, gold hair wind-whipped into serpentine coils. Her face must have been set slightly above the face of the Virgin of Guadalupe, because there was that eye again, that exact same (never to be expunged?) misaligned eye, peeking out, lurking like a woeful Adam's apple, a wound, high in the beach girl's throat.

What did it signify, this half-hidden face? Here was no miracle, but a piece of mischief. (It's the story that makes the miracle, isn't it?) Yet, what was any of this to me? Why should I, of all people, feel mocked?

I needed more sleep, I kept coming back to this. Optimally, eight hours when I'd been averaging five to six—max. I'd tried all the advertised remedies: sleep mask, ear plugs, an antisnore protector I pasted on the bridge of my nose (in case the sound of my own snoring was the culprit)—nothing helped. I didn't want to start taking pills, though; I was all too familiar with where that led. Aside from long walks, what I needed was a hobby, tinkering or woodwork or stamp-collecting, something . . . anything to re-direct my thoughts. *Anything* to get my mind off its same old same old obsessional round, that well-worn treadmill.

If only there'd been a word from Michael—

18

Passing

The IRT, 168th Street: the light in the station was sepia, dreamlike, a murky place for murky goings-on. I was on my way to a funeral parlor in the Bronx. Barely more than a month after he'd been assigned a cell and cellmates, Gary had been stomped to death in a brawl. (Hokey pokey, with a vengeance, I couldn't help thinking.) Word was that he'd provoked the attack—it sounded all too plausible. From the time I'd first met Gary, I'd known that he was brimming with anger, but since I never felt myself in personal danger, I'd failed to take him seriously enough. I'd realized too late that his resorting to a gun, even a toy as he'd done at first, had been a shout for attention, an SOS unheeded. He'd been asking—crying out, really—to be stopped.

Karina had been sensitive enough not to belabor any of this—we've all had our casualties—and she'd granted me a time-release to attend the funeral. I would have welcomed company, but everyone in the office was so pressed, I didn't bother to ask around. Besides, I was the only person on the staff who'd gone one-on-one with Gary over an extended period of time.

Aside from misgivings over how inattentive I'd been (that now-unforgettable business of heads falling off) at my last meeting with Gary, what was I feeling?

Numb, maybe, but that could have been nothing but an excuse, a euphemism for feeling nothing. In truth, I'd never warmed to Gary.

I was more depressed than sad—depressed in general—Gary's business simply reinforcing a preexisting condition. Add to that: lonely, yet sealed off from others—strange to myself. Those weird moments when my own tongue lay heavy in my mouth, heavy and strange—inedible meat. I knew it wasn't normal.

It was well before rush hour, plenty of seats, the train half-empty. Everyone glanced up when, like a burst of summer sunshine, two girls entered. They were dressed unseasonably in yellow and pink halter tops and skirts so scant they might have been underpants. You couldn't miss them, since they chose to remain standing, hanging on to the center pole. The fatter one slipped down the straps of her halter and bared herself to the waist, calling out, "Better get a look now! Before the police come."

Heads dipped. *See no evil: keep those lids shut, you never saw a thing.* Safest policy in subways, elevators, buses, pressed up all too closely against strangers and strange intentions. *You never know.*

Curiosity got the better of me, though. With my head lowered, eyes half shut, I managed to peek without staring. I saw. They weren't particularly spectacular breasts, although the nipples were unusually large, ovoid. Then I closed my eyes for real, embarrassed for the girl. Don't know when she covered up again or if she bothered. Needless to say, the police never showed.

I made it to the funeral parlor in time to sign the book of remembrance set up in the vestibule. Only a handful of mourners had arrived as yet, so I occupied myself with reading over the entries before mine. There wasn't a single name I recognized, but I did spot two O'Briens, same as Gary's family name.

Piped organ muzak as we entered. Finding an inconspicuous seat close to the door, I settled in. I plucked one of the memorial flyers from the pew rack; it told me less, and other, than what I already knew. Most of the mourners were clustered in the back and seemed reluctant to move when urged to come and fill the empty pews up front. I shuffled forward, sheepishly, along with the rest—a handful of strangers, doing our best to look grim for decency's sake.

All together, we couldn't even fill the reserved section intended for members of the immediate family.

I studied the single floral spray. Mostly white flowers; it doesn't matter what kind, I don't like flowers anywhere or anytime. Lilies, roses, carnations, gardenias, make no difference—all they do is stir up my allergies.

We stood, sat, stood again.

The preacher, or speaker, or whatever the man was, gave a little sermon, doling out a dollop of despair, then a dollop of hope, and sending us forth to do battle. It reminded me of every graduation speech I've ever heard. Clearly, he didn't know Gary from Adam. Gary may have been many things, but "a gentle soul"? Please!

Still, I made an effort to concentrate and conjure up a mood appropriate to the occasion. For me, most especially, this should have been a time of reflection and contrition. The kindest thing that could be said about my handling of his case was that I'd been inattentive. In fact, I'd been bored and often angry with Gary. (This happens with certain individuals, it's a matter of personal chemistry.) I should have acknowledged these facts and passed his case along to someone who might have felt differently and worked with him more effectively.

Coulda, shoulda, woulda, mighta . . . June was right. Michael had usurped all my attention—it wasn't fair to anyone else. I had to "move on"—had to "get a life," as she'd say. And I resolved to do so. Starting then and there, facing Gary's open casket, his face and hands the color of pewter (there'd been no embalming), I made a promise to myself to live while I had the privilege, and in particular: (a) to find a nearby gym and work out on the machines twice a week, (b) to take in a movie once a week, and (c) to enjoy a leisurely restaurant meal while I was at it, avoiding takeout.

We shuffled out from the chapel to an old Irish blessing, bidding the road rise up to meet Gary, the wind be always at his back. The afternoon was bright and breezy, a frontal, slapping wind rising to meet us as we stepped into the open. The strong sun was a solvent, though, for any lingering traces of gloom. I didn't stick around for the drive out to the cemetery; I hope someone did.

I didn't give a thought to Michael all the way back (except for briefly noting that I wasn't thinking about him), and it seemed to be working until a panhandler, a wizened black fellow wearing a padded parka with the hood up, snow boots, and woolen gloves with cutaway fingers, rattled a tin cup filled with coins in my face, whispering "mercy . . ." I rummaged in my coat pocket for whatever I could turn up in the way of quarters and dimes—not much, and useless, I knew—the kind of sop to conscience I usually did my best to resist. I felt no better for the gesture, nor did he seem much impressed after I scratched around in various inner pockets, coming up mostly with pennies, which he waved away contemptuously, as if adding insult to injury and not worth the effort of taking.

I was in for a shock on my return, the waiting room so dazzling that, for an instant, I couldn't tell whether the figure framed by the window was standing with his face or back to me.

It was Michael.

Since I hadn't known when I'd be back from Gary's funeral, I'd moved around appointments, clearing my entire afternoon calendar. I was free to invite Michael into my office. He settled himself in his usual chair without ceremony, placing his backpack between his feet. It was bulkier, I noticed, than before. Understandably— since living out on the street meant toting everything he needed around with him wherever he went.

"Well, well . . ." I began, then bit my tongue and waited.

He surprised me (yet another surprise) by coming right to the point: "Can you get me back in St. Joe's?"

I said I'd try, I couldn't promise.

"Don't count on it," I cautioned, echoing some of Father Evans's favorite phrases about fitting in, getting along, and assuming adult responsibility. "You'll play by the rules from here on?"

Michael nodded agreeably. I knew he'd been through this song and dance many times in his short life. I wondered, fleetingly, why he was holding his head at what had to be an uncomfortable angle.

All in all, he seemed not that much the worse for wear. He was thinner than before, I thought, though with all the layers he had on, it was hard to say for sure. His outer sweatshirt was frayed, his chinos soiled, but these were unimportant details—mere externals.

"I'm going to try and get along," he said, and I resolved to do what I could.

I didn't want to get his hopes up only to dash them, so again I reminded him, "All I can do is try." And I sent him around the corner with a coupon for a hamburger and soft drink while I telephoned.

Father Evans wasn't as intransigent as I'd expected.

"He can't have his old room back, in any case," he said. "But I'll set up a cot in the common room for tonight. It's the best I can do for the time being. Tomorrow—after we have a serious talk—we'll see. I'll see . . ."

Michael smiled when he heard this. As he turned, I realized that he'd been holding his head at a certain angle to hide the imprint of bruises. They were at the green and yellowing stage, which meant old and fading, yet, once noticed, impossible to ignore.

"Rough out there?" I ventured.

He let out a big sigh.

I'd have given anything to know where he'd been but judged it better not to ask. "Around," would be all the answer I'd get. Most likely, he'd simply clam up.

I didn't want to spoil the mood. So I didn't press—simply set up an appointment with him later in the week. I meant to move slowly and whittle my questions down to the ones that really mattered.

Hard to believe how relieved I felt.

19

Scheming

Karina summoned me into her office the next morning. There was, she assured me, "nothing in particular" she had in mind. She'd been calling in "all the troops" one by one, an opportunity to talk freely.

I must have looked puzzled—or guilty.

"No problems?" she said.

I shrugged. "None but the usual."

"Lucky you," she said.

Out with it!—I wanted her to come to the point. But I waited.

She'd been going over records, double-checking all cases, all clients, she explained, stressing the "all."

"Procedures, procedures, procedures!"—the chant was familiar. "My supervisor is breathing down my neck, his supervisor down his. We've got to work by the book. Stick to the protocols. Follow the procedures step by step. No shortcuts, no going by gut instinct. Things may be getting a little lax around here. I'm not singling you out—"

Oh, no? She took such pains to speak in generalities, I couldn't help suspecting that she'd heard something particular about Michael.

The fact was, I hadn't "set goals" or come up with an appropriate "intervention." I'd never set a projected "date of termination." I was still hovering between steps one and two of the canonical seven, somewhere between "initial contact" and "relationship building."

In truth, I couldn't have been more guilty of the irregularities Karina mentioned. Michael was way past termination under the old or new (post–budget cuts) dispensation. He should have been marked "inactive" and dispatched to the Dead File weeks ago. So I knew I had to act fast and keep my plans to myself.

I'd started thinking about active intervention in Michael's case. It would involve footwork, as well as paper and online search. I ought to have started on this long ago . . . But, then again, supposing I were way off base in my hunch, my leap—again and again I had to remind myself that I had nothing solid or proven to stand on.

After all, I hadn't gotten Michael to confide anything—anything at all—to me so far. I'd have to confront him first, trick him, if need be, into admitting that he believed his mother was feeding him, and for some reason (explore the why of this?) not feeding him directly, but resorting to drop-offs all over the city.

These would be only the first steps.

Then, after that: Locate his mother. (If possible—everything hinged on my being able to find her.) Arrange to meet with her privately. Assess her condition and whether a further meeting, bringing Michael along, would be at all feasible.

And then, if all went well, bring Michael to meet his mother face-to-face—a dose of reality, after which, his bluff called, his delusion in shreds, he might begin to see the world as it is and come to terms with it. In short: begin to grow up.

That was my plan, the bare scheme. Risky, to say the least. It struck me as madness in certain lights, the only sanity, in others. There was the whole question of efficacy—of possible losses versus possible gains. And, of course, there was the matter of proper procedure. But who dithers about protocol with a man overboard?

It would be for his own good.

❖

One more thing—a positive development. ("On the personal level," as people say.) Although I took my suppers alone, I set my place with care. I attended to what I was eating: I took the time to put down a plate. Now, as before, it was mainly takeout. But no more eating out of paper cartons.

Napkin in a tidy triangle. Fork on the napkin, to the left; knife and spoon on the right. June, at least, would be impressed.

I read the nutrition columns, picked complex carbohydrates over the simple, favored the folates.

No gobbling. I took tiny bites, chewed them up fine. No more lukewarm. Food meant to be eaten hot was eaten hot; cold—cold. I tried to taste before I swallowed, to savor as it went down.

And yet it was all enforced ritual; food hadn't tasted right to me for some time. Maybe I simply wasn't hungry, knowing that I was filled beyond my need. It kind of spoiled my appetite to be sitting there eating and think that someone (someone known to me) had been eating my garbage. Wouldn't it you?

Something else not so good: I was back to smoking. It wasn't yet a compulsion. I could stop the next minute if I had to, I told myself. A cigarette after dinner was a civilized custom. So I leaned back and breathed, slowly, deeply. I attended to the hum, the heartbeat of the refrigerator—a sympathetic vibration, if I chose to think of it that way.

I chose to think of it that way.

I kept starting these letters to June—

"It's been winter since you left me" . . . was how one of these beauties began.

One was perfectly crazy:

"You never let me speak" . . . As if she'd been talking to me nonstop during her absence. As if I'd been trying (wanting) to explain myself. Another went, "Together we" . . . That was as far as I got. Together we'd *what*? I hadn't the foggiest where I was going with that one.

Whatever. Jottings like these, the crumpled bits and pieces of my days, ended up in what we at the office called "the round file." With their points conceded and promises made, these beginnings of letters never sent were more than doodles, more than empty scraps. However garbled, however unsustainable, they were pledges of effort, of good intention, and—for the moment—sincerely meant.

20

Intervention

I rang up Father Evans with news of my plan.

"I see," Father Evans said. I'd met the man face-to-face briefly on only two occasions, but I knew he was closing his eyes as he said this, it's how he sees.

Then, "I don't know. On the one hand, Michael isn't showing up for meals again, and, by now, we all know what that means. He hasn't latched on to anyone here—his social skills are nil. So it's the same old stalemate and somebody has to do something. On the other—"

He didn't have to spell out the objections. Once I'd formulated my plan for intervention, I'd come up with plenty of counterarguments of my own. Suppose Michael's mother was leading a new life, married with other kids, her troubled past well behind her? Suppose I did locate his mother under her old name: Would she consent to see me? Would she hear me out? Would she finally agree to meet with Michael? Would she be capable of understanding why this was so important for him? Would Michael submit to my plan? Would I have to trick him into coming along?

And if—after all those other ifs—I did manage to get mother and son together, how would such a reunion go? Wouldn't it amount to shock therapy for Michael? A massive assault on all he held dear?

The risk was huge.

But what choice did I have, really? I'd held back long enough. This was my last-ditch effort, a chance I had to take. I kept my plan secret from others in the office, knowing full well that I should have at least consulted Karina. She was my supervisor, after all. But uneasy as I was about going it alone, once I decided to act, I was determined to let nothing—no mere protocol—stand in my way.

There *had* to be intervention, and it had to take place without delay.

The surprising thing (the one detail I'd never anticipated) was that it wasn't all that difficult to find his mother. Why had no one thought of it before? I found the same name as on her first hospitalization records, same date for first child born. Steady persistence (and interest) was all it required to unearth these details. There were years unaccounted for in the seventies and eighties, but she certainly seemed to be one and the same person. I used the Department of Public Welfare records and two private computer tracking services, vitalrec and AutoTrackXP, paying for them out of personal funds. I couldn't believe my luck: all the available information meshed.

There was another child, I learned, a daughter on record. She'd been adopted out, successfully, and the family had gone out of state, out of my jurisdiction—none of my business, anyway.

I needed to let off steam somehow and confided my plan to June. She was predictably negative: "You've no right to play God" was how she put it.

"I must get to the bottom of this!"

"*Must* you? Know what I think? You're jealous of Michael—"

"Jealous—you crazy? Jealous of *what*?"

"His conviction—he won't be shaken loose from it. You ask me what I think—I think you're meddling big-time."

I knew the risks, but my mind was made up. No one could have faulted me for lack of conviction then.

I did slow myself down a bit, though. Here I was in hot pursuit of the mother when I hadn't gotten to first base with Michael—his secrecy the sting in the ointment. Securing his confession would have to be the next step after my searching out the mother. The mother came first because I needed to have evidence that she existed, that she had nothing to do with his Dumpster dining, and that she'd be willing to cooperate in disabusing him of any illusion on that score. I was more and more convinced that coming clean on the Dumpster business was essential for Michael's sanity and for his physical health—a question of life or death. There would be no point in continuing without it.

So, first—to nail down the mother.

21

SRO

An ill-omened ride. It all started when I boarded an unmarked subway train. I tried to check before it set off, asking twice, "Is this the A-train?"—receiving one grunt and one dour "hope so" by way of reassurance—and decided to risk it.

As soon as the doors closed, a shout went up: "Great Bob almighty! They're chopping him in pieces." The carriage doors, closing automatically, were caught on the arm of a latecomer trying to worm his way in—one arm, pinned at the elbow, inside the carriage; the other, relentlessly pounding metal on the outside. Quite a commotion. Then the door opened, but only enough to disgorge the trapped arm, and the train moved on.

Not five minutes later, wouldn't you know it, the lights went out. In pitch dark between stations, the train shuddered to a halt. There was an inhuman crackle over what passed for a public address system: sounds pitched at us: an announcement in some sort of creole of Spanish, Yiddish, Ebonics—a little Korean and Bulgarian thrown in for good measure. All I could make out was the word "indication," and that only by guessing—"indication" (I later learned) being code for "trouble ahead." We never found out what that trouble was. In ignorance, we inched on to the next station, to be evacuated there; in bewilderment, we gawked as our train moved past us—empty now and still dark—on to points unknown. We waited, unable to do anything but stare at the mouth of the tunnel into which the train had disappeared, or kill time by pacing the platform. Tags for the "Parricides—Tony, Alonzo, and Jimmy the Tiger," were splattered in big, bloated letters over three panels of wall. I wasn't late yet but couldn't help grudging the minutes ticking away.

When the next train arrived, we all tried to squeeze in first. From the moment the door opened, I had my eye on the last remaining vacant seat, but lost to a young woman who lunged and elbowed her way to it. I couldn't let well enough alone (though I wasn't tired and she probably wasn't, either) and I chose to stand right in front of her, to grip and glower down at her from an already-crowded pole, where I had to struggle for a handhold, had to twist my way in finger by finger, the whole business senseless. But that's how we do things in the great city.

Although I arrived on time and found my destination without further incident, it was an inauspicious start to what I knew could only be, at best, a difficult visit.

She was living in a walk-up apartment in one of those single-room occupancy hotels (called "SROs," for short), decayed, but once elegant, structures salvaged by the city for public assistance housing. Honeyless honeycombs, is how I think of them, the landlords divvying up the buildings into innumerable closet-sized apartments. Shared bathrooms and kitchens in the hallways. Back in the seventies when mental patients on medication were released from warehousing in state hospitals and turned loose on the streets, many of them had to be warehoused again in SROs. The particular building in which Michael's mother lived was far from the worst of these. It still maintained an entrance awning and its upscale name—The Cranford—but its corridors smelled of urine and disinfectant. Inside was gloomy enough. The walls were grime-gray, with dark (institutional green) borders; even with all the lights in the hallway burning, there was no way you could tell it was mid-morning outside.

"I don't remember you," she said by way of greeting.

"You never met me before," I explained, but she wasn't having it.

"You all say that," she said.

Her apartment was little more than a cubbyhole, so cramped it would be hard to avoid sitting knee to knee. I'd been desperately curious to get a good look at her. Now I wanted a safe distance and decided against the loveseat (the only upholstered chair), choosing instead one of her metal folding chairs.

Once seated, I panicked; I'd lost all sense of having a script worked out beforehand. Here I was, face-to-face with Michael's mother, Elizabeth, the living, breathing, actual person. I realized that I had no idea what *her* lines would be; any script prepared in advance was bound to be a monologue and useless.

In much the same pattern as Michael, Elizabeth had wandered before resettling in New York. Her meanderings could be traced through Social Welfare agency records from Akron, Ohio, and Joplin, Missouri, and from as far west as Oklahoma City. Official reports had it that she'd been functioning reasonably well in recent years, currently working in a Goodwill center, doing something semi-skilled—I want to say with lampshades, but I'm not sure . . . something, I forget just what, to do with preparing, or repairing, donated goods for resale in thrift shops, and that she'd held it for a number of years.

Impossible not to feel claustrophobic inside that apartment. For one thing, it was hard to breathe: there seemed to be some sort of floral spray in the air, a loud fragrance. And the only view of the outside world was through a small, heavily barred, shut window, facing a brick wall. Despite two locks and a chain-bolt on her door, the scars from past break-ins were all too visible. The tiny bed-sitting-dining room was crowded, with one of those half-size refrigerators you find in college dormitories, hot plate and sink, a bridge table covered in leatherette, two folding chairs, and a tiny rabbit-eared television kept running all the while I was there. A few small decorative touches: the geranium on the sill with an aluminum foil skirt dressing the pot, two china dogs alongside, one black, one white. A photograph torn from a calendar, taped over the refrigerator door, had a pair of giraffes grazing treetops, necks intertwined, a waterfall cascading in thick drapery folds behind them. There were no personal photos that I could see.

The woman was maddening—her vagueness. When I asked her how her family was doing, a look of strained perplexity crossed her face. "What family?" her voice almost a whisper. "No skin off your back," she added in stronger voice. She regarded me head-on then and struck me as perfectly sane. But then, in a heartbeat, she was on to playing the madwoman. "It's gas usually makes them cry, all it is. Anyhow that's so long ago . . . Lived in Astoria don't know how long, then in Flushing. I lose track, my head's clogged up." Then—another about-face: back to sane and sober. She turned on me a canny look. "Who sent you?"

I'd prepared for this much, concocting a nonexistent supervisor, but before I could get the name out—I'm not a good liar—my breath snagged. I paused a second to clear my throat. She rushed in, sparing me: "Everybody lying to me all the time! Don't give me that. Berthoff sent you but I don't know why, what he wants now. Better watch out—he's listening, he hears everything we say."

"I have no idea what you're talking about," I protested.

"Everybody says that!"

She was having none of it. "It's Berthoff, can't fool me. Or Bergdof, like that schmancy store. Same difference. He goes by a whole bunch of phony names, it's never only the one. I know he's not a real doctor, and I know he sent you here. He's the one with the mustache that turns up at the corners—like horns. Never said what his real business was . . . Anyway, I know he sent you, he's into everything. He knows when I been bad or good—he—"

"That's Santa—you mean Santa." I couldn't resist. She gave me a frosty look.

Nobody could claim she'd had an easy life. With her lined forehead, her bracketed mouth, she looked older than her forty-two years.

It was her day off; she wore a housecoat, fuzzy slippers, no makeup. Her hair, dyed red, black and gray at the roots, fell in greasy strands. In spite of all the wear and tear, I couldn't dismiss the resemblance to Michael. It was in her eyes—unmistakable—the indeterminate color (or maybe, in both cases, my never getting close enough to determine what color exactly), whether pale blue or gray, and the wide-apart, spacious set of them, the shared wondering gaze they cast upon the world. A look of invincible innocence, I'd be tempted to say, although in her case it wouldn't really apply. The resemblance was also noticeable in her features, mouth and nose, the cast of her face: less clear-edged than Michael's, a bit blurred as if shaken by the passage of years.

It was terribly awkward. Whenever I fumbled, the television seeped in to fill the gap, and I lost whatever thread our conversation might have followed. Added to everything else, I didn't know how to sit, where to place my feet, what to do with my arms, or whether to smile, wondering whether I'd be smiling in the middle of my face if I did—afraid my smile would betray me by slanting off to one side. Talk about two-faced! When I tried to project steady friendliness—neither smile nor smirk, simply sympathetic interest—my cheek twitched with the effort. I doubt any of this was lost on her.

Enough of preliminaries—time to get down to business: "You have a son . . . know where he is now?"

I'd resolved not to mention the daughter unless she herself brought it up.

"No skin off your back," she said a second time. "Easy for you to say."

I let these remarks pass. It seemed to me (maybe I imagined it, her teeth were too perfect) that I heard the soft after-clack of dentures when she spoke.

Everything was atremble between us now. I heard one television anchor saying to another, "That's a *great* question." I had no idea what the question was. I was trying my best to concentrate yet didn't dare mention the television, assuming it was a kind of barely heard background music to her, white noise necessary to keeping her calm, an accompaniment to breathing, nothing more. But when a drumbeat, an actual drumbeat, for something or other came on, I had all I could do to keep from leaping to my feet and throttling the thing. *One swift twist,* I thought. And immediately after, *Don't you dare,* the thread between us so tenuous I couldn't take my attention off her for a second.

". . . Government took him off her hands." *Her* hands? Come again? Adroitly, she'd shifted to third person, as if this had nothing to do with her. "Doctor says they're better off." She gave a small throat-clearing cough. "That's what they told her."

"But that doesn't prevent you from visiting with them, does it?" No use beating around the bush—I plunged. "How'd you like to see your son? He's a young man now—twenty-eight. A fine young man."

"My so-called son?"

"Devoted young man," I added.

"Devoted?"

"To you."

"To you?" She smiled in no particular direction, then sobered and asked, "Can you still see the scar?"

Then—it's funny what you do at times like that—I actually caught myself staring, as if trying to guess where the scar might be.

"If I could bring him to you."

"Here?" She stiffened.

"Wherever. Any place you'd prefer to meet."

"At The Dorado you could choose your own menu. You could lie down whenever you wanted."

"Wherever you want to meet is fine with me."

"Just walk right up and say hi—that the idea? Little friendly get-together?"

"It'd be awkward at first, but I'd introduce you. Stay with the two of you long as you want. It would be good for both of you. Think about it, give it a little time, don't say yes or no right away. I'll call you—call the manager's desk, I mean. That's how you do it here, right?"

"Gotta get my own phone."

"I'll get in touch with you through the manager in the meantime."

"It's not right."

"What's not?"

"Living in this shithole. People all gobbed up together. Banging on the pipes night and day. I been mugged—how many times? I can't lock the door to the toilet. They crap in the bathtub. In the bathtub! Like animals! Everywhere you look, it's all decrapitated! There's this cokehead drops his spikes in the hall. Gotta get away—"

"I'll see what I can do," and I made the mistake of sneaking a glance at my watch.

"Money, money, money," she mocked, "better get going." Then her attention shifted to the television screen, to an ad for mortgage loans, a fat man frantic, digging for a paper lost and buried somewhere on his desk.

"Lost another loan to Di-Tech!" the fat man moaned.

Entrance music for one of the soaps came on.

"I'm willing to give you all the time you need."

"Yeah, sure. I bet. Anyways, like I said, gotta get outta here. Call the cops and nobody does nothing. Mind my own business, anybody let me . . ."

"I'll look into it."

"I'm short this month, see. Gas and light—they're warning me. Got a couch on layaway—"

"Tell me what you need to get through the month."

She assured me a hundred would barely cover things.

I doled out forty. ("Enough to make a cat laugh," I thought I heard her mutter under her breath.)

I was all too aware that money changing hands like this was strictly out of bounds. My hands shook not only from nervousness but from trying to contain my anger that she had manipulated me to this extent. "That's it—all I have," I lied. While she counted and double-counted the wad with expert fingers, I could not help but reflect how "alert and oriented" she seemed to be, how canny, how sane.

"More when you've met him," I promised. "I'll give you a buzz." But then I added, inexplicably—that itch in my throat again— "Put on your curls! It's going to happen."

Her last words startled me: "D'you have any idea what you're asking? I don't know him." And, for once, she looked me straight in the eye, dead on.

"That must change," I answered, with all the conviction I could muster.

Out on the street, I savored my release. I decided to walk for a bit then catch a cab to the next subway stop. The neighborhood, never affluent but once decent, was clearly going to the dogs. Buy now—pay later was the theme. Instant check cashing (no credit required, no questions asked), a pawnshop on every block, liquor stores, closet-sized bodegas. Sidewalk vendors everywhere, peddling lifted wares. Signs merged: PRAISALS GIRLS! GIRLS! GIRLS! LAS CHICAS! COMPRA, VENDA, RENTA!—a stew! But I couldn't escape what I was trying so hard not to think about: I hadn't the least grasp of what I'd set in motion. Suppose I did succeed in getting mother and son to meet, sit down and share a meal, what then? What could such a meeting mean? Some sort of communion—a breaking and sharing of bread? A reunion? How would they even begin? What on earth could they find to say to one another? Who was delusional now?

And yet—I kept coming back to this—the get-together I was working to bring off, even if forced, meant *doing* something at last, taking some action, breaking the stalemate of merely sitting and waiting—waiting which had to end one way or another. Making this effort meant motion, not stasis, any kind of movement better than none.

Of course, I'd been completely unprofessional. I'd crossed a line, no question. Michael's mother was not one of my clients. There had to be a social worker assigned to her, checking up on her from month to month. Then again, I was all too aware of how such arrangements fared in practice. A social worker with an enormous caseload of aging clients long on the public dole would have to treat a case like this mainly as a bookkeeping problem. Questions of unreported income and social security fraud would be the prime concerns, not much else.

Still . . . to play it safe, I should have located the social worker assigned to her and at least gone through the motions of professional consultation.

Not only was I acting solo and out of bounds, interfering with someone else's client, but I'd been prejudiced from the start, I'd chosen sides—*his,* not hers. However many times I told myself, *I cannot judge her,* I did. I knew I was being unfair: mother and son were both clients of the social welfare system. Each had a story, a sad personal history. Michael's mother, too, had never known her real parents. She'd been a runaway from an orphanage and from her single foster care placement, out on the streets and on her own, from the time she was twelve. She, too, might be called a victim. Yet the stubborn fact remained: I disliked the woman. I'd been predisposed not to like her before I'd ever laid eyes on her. Once met, I had no desire to see her ever again, and yet—this was the kicker—I'd committed myself to bending every effort toward that very thing. My resolve was granite.

22

Showdown

"I'm listening," I said, and I paused for as long as I could stand it.

"Guess I'm having a conversation with myself . . ."

Michael, staring out the window, said nothing to dispute this.

"There's no point continuing," I went on as calmly as I could, "unless you let me in on things. If you're not in a talking mood, you can simply answer yes or no. You don't even have to say the words—just nod for yes and shake your head for no. Otherwise, I quit. That's the deal."

If Michael consented, he gave no clue.

"I'm trying to get this straight. You guess . . . it seems like . . . you *believe* . . . that your mother is feeding you from Dumpsters, that right? Am I getting warm? For some reason, you've bound yourself to thinking and acting this way . . ."

Still stonewalling. Gaze level, face impassive, he stared in silence at the window behind me.

I wanted to shake him—shake the secret out of him.

"I still don't get it—which is it? You *imagine*? You prefer? You want to think that your mother leaves food for you?"

"I know she does!"

Of course he knew no such thing—I'd backed him into a corner. But I could hardly believe my ears: his words were tantamount to a confession. I did my best to keep my voice level. "How? How do you know?"

He answered calmly, "You see I am fed."

"Like a dog!" The words rushed out of me.

"I am fed," he repeated, only this time tears sprang to his eyes.

Good, I thought, *I'm getting through to him.* And I pressed on.

"Sure you are . . . With rats! Roaches! Infected needles!"

I couldn't afford to lose momentum now that I had his attention. "You *wish* you were fed! But wishing doesn't make it so. You know what the word *delusion* means? Know that delusion can kill?"

Then, suddenly, he tore open his backpack and, rummaging for something at the bottom, started to spill the contents onto my desk.

"No—that won't be necessary . . . it isn't helpful . . . put that away! I won't be distracted." I'd lost all pretense of calm.

He gathered up his things so quickly that I never saw what it was he meant to show me. Some item of "proof," no doubt.

"I've got to close your case unless you stop this nonsense. *Now.*" It was no lie. "We've gone on too long without my knowing the first thing. I'm trying to help—"

And—nothing.

"Okay!" Two can play this. *Not another word from me,* I resolved, and busied myself at my desk, stacking loose papers, closing his file folder, patting the cover shut and resting both hands on top, as if to say, *That's it—*

I even went through the charade of pushing back my chair, readying to stand.

Then the words were flung at me: "It's real! I know."

"How real?" I pounced.

"As real as you . . . seeing you now . . . as me sitting here . . . ," his voice dwindled, "real as anything . . ."

"You don't sound convinced. You *half*-believe, then?"

One last try—"The thing I've never understood . . . is why the drop-offs? Why would she do this? Why don't you and your mom simply get together and eat? What's keeping you?"

His lips closed over a perfect nougat of silence.

"There's nothing keeping you," I went on. "I've met your mom. She's eager to meet with you." Then, with desperate improvisation, "Ever think she might be tired of having to make the rounds of the Dumpsters day after day trying to keep you fed? Trying to guess where you might show up . . . Maybe she wants to talk to you about it. Don't you owe her that courtesy?"

He stared at me blankly.

I was reminded of another client—Fritz Reiner—at our last session, years ago. He was a learned man, and I thought I'd been so clever in finding him out: I finally felt confident enough to interpret the dream that kept troubling him. He listened impassively, made no comment at first. When I said that he seemed "abstracted," he corrected me: "*Sub*tracted, rather . . . It seems I am still in the box, the same box. You're saying this was also in my dream. Suppose I pinch myself, what does that prove? I could be pinching myself in my dream . . . We were sitting exactly so, in the dream and now. That shade torn in the corner, the sun in my eyes, exactly so . . ." And he went on talking, as if to himself: "I must still be dreaming—dreaming that I woke up and dressed and kept my appointment to hear you say these same words, exactly the same words you are saying now . . ."

The dream was airtight; I could do nothing.

I'd no idea what became of Reiner since. A therapeutic failure, it should have served fair warning. What had I learned from it? Nothing, apparently. Once started with Michael, nothing was going to stop me. "I could arrange a get-together," I said. "I could take you there. And then I'd leave you. Or stick around if you want—whatever's comfortable. The important thing is, you can sit down and eat together, decent food in a decent place." And then I pushed it. "How about our next appointment time? I'll give her a call and make arrangements. If there's any hitch, I'll let you know. Otherwise—we have a date this time next week."

Michael blanched. His lips moved soundlessly.

"I wish it could be sooner—the sooner we get all this behind us, the better," I said, cutting off further discussion. As soon as the words were out, I realized how carelessly revealing they were, how much I wanted to wash my hands of the situation.

Michael lurched to his feet, his face stricken, scrambled for his backpack, and fled.

Shock tactics. I knew I should have spoken with great care, the utmost restraint, but such niceties were beyond me. How desperately I wanted this whole business to be over! But I'd committed myself to slow haste. Haste—because we hadn't the luxury of time for Michael to get used to the idea more gradually. Slow—because, much as I wanted to be done with this, I wasn't willing to speed up the process by arranging for a get-together after office hours. Adjusting my appointments to create an open-ended time slot was going to take some doing.

Why insist on official hours?

I wanted to remain aboveboard, placing my intervention where it belonged, within the therapeutic framework.

Let the record reflect this.

23

Bat Light

To live as a mollusk would be nice . . .

Why not give up? I kept urging myself. It was that simple. Let Michael eat whatever he wanted—rat poison, if that's what he wanted. *Whatever!* He was an adult, after all.

But then I wondered—wasn't all my self-argument a devious way of keeping Michael in my sights, another way of never letting go?

To say that I was "at loose ends" did not begin to describe my disarray.

Hungry for distraction, I watched television until my eyes burned. I rearranged the magnets on my refrigerator, phoned Weather, even called Dial-A-Prayer six or seven times, getting nothing but a steady, implacable bleeping in reply. Finally, at wit's end, I forced myself out to a singles bar.

Do they still call them "dives"? They should. The place was subterranean, a cave, the light muddy, men and women navigating by sexual sonar or colliding hit-and-miss.

I groped my way to an empty barstool. Doing my best to sound practiced and casual, I ordered a Heineken and swiveled round to meet my neighbor, a girl with wild electroshock hair, a deliberately mussed-up style I think they call "hair storm," or "bed head."

It was she who broke the ice. "My dog died," she said and swiped at the corner of her eye.

"Sorry to hear it," I said.

"Sure. Sure you are." She lifted her drink then set it down untasted. "You sound sorry. Like you care. Anyhow, don't. He's in doggie heaven by now."

I had nothing to say to this.

"Haven't I seen you before? Your face looks so familiar . . ."

"People always say that," I agreed. "It's the symmetry: two eyes, two ears. One nose, one mouth, more or less central . . . But it's so dark, how can you tell?"

"I love this song," she answered and took my hand and led me onto the dance floor. No point protesting: *Can't dance!* The only time I tried, it was lessons, my mother made me, and it was slide-slide-clomp-slide-clomp—box steps—nothing like what I was seeing here. Here, I could swear, there were dancers swimming in air, leaping with torches, beating the ground with sticks. No one led and no one followed.

I lost her and moved on. What happened next is dark to me. All I remember is a ring of fire, the light intermittent, writhing shadows, the suction fierce, the pot roiling—and I, beside myself, red meat and fire . . .

I flogged the air—lunged, thrashed, twined, galloped—

"Down! Down! Down! The flames grow higher!" Pounding on the downbeat. I sweated, heat beating upward from my footsoles—the floor was burning. I buckled, shaking, shaking loose from my bones—when someone, mouthing O-O-O some something, broke out of the circle, cutting a path to me . . . *Steady there* . . . I needed a wall to press against to brace myself—

The floor would not stay put . . .

. . . When it came to rest at last, we stood, each on a little square of linoleum; our hands semaphored, island to island. Felt like I was going to pass out. She towed me over to the nearest chair and there I flumped, head to table. She hovered. "Hey . . . Remember me? You feeling *better!*"—bending low to catch my reply.

146

"Think so." Lifting my head ever so slowly. "Semi-steady." (Semi-solid, really.) "Not used to this."

"Well, relax, take a deep breath. I'll get us some beers."

We sipped in silence to start. A powerful thirst was upon me.

"How about now?" she asked. "Better?"

I assured her I was.

"You should have seen yourself—what you looked like—"

"Like what?"

"Like you were being attacked by killer bees. This place is for dancing, why'd you come?"

I told her I'd read an ad in the paper: "'Paradise Alley . . . It's So *Now!*' . . . Thought I'd see what 'now' means."

I was struck by the tight black jersey she wore, not so much by the thrust of breast beneath, as by its surface, the glitter of particles fine as a sprinkling of salt dusting her shoulders . . . Curious . . . a sort of radiant dandruff. I was about to reach over and brush the particles away when I realized they were decoration, meant to stay, and checked myself.

"What are you thinking?" she asked.

"What am I thinking?" *Was I thinking?* "Who says I'm thinking?" A new song was playing. Something about a tear and a beer, tears falling in beer. "You were saying?" she said.

"Saying?" I stared at her dark lips. What had I wanted to say?

I'd started jingling the coins in my pocket. She must have taken this as a cue for my being ready to pay up and depart, and somehow imagined that I'd invited her to come with me, but before I had time to catch on and rectify her misunderstanding, she'd slithered down from her barstool, saying, "Be back in a dot!" and headed off to the powder room. It was only after she left that I stooped to tighten a dangling shoelace and took a good look at my feet; I was wearing white socks! They glowed, even in the shadows you couldn't miss them. White socks were only acceptable for sports—otherwise, a dead giveaway that the man wearing them was starting to slide and it would be all downhill from there. That was the received wisdom on socks, according to

June. I still heard June in my mind, still felt her chewing on me.
So the white socks did it—I scrammed, I didn't wait around.

After this fiasco, after vowing *never again*, did I seriously con-
sider dropping in at the massage parlor on Eighth Avenue for
the "rub and tug" they advertised? I did, I toyed with the idea,
then promptly forgot about it. Instead, I invited one of the new
social work interns out to supper at a Chinese restaurant not far
from the office, a place I'd never been to before. Oh, she was nice
enough, but I couldn't rise to the occasion. Faced with the unfamiliar menu, I stalled; the words dissolved into gibberish. "What
is recommended?" I appealed to the waiter. "All is recommended,"
he said. I passed my menu over to the girl. "You better be the one
to choose for both of us." And I left almost the entire burden of
conversation for her to carry, as well.

When dessert came, we broke open our fortune cookies. Hers
read, "An introduction will alter your plans."

There wasn't even a scrap of blank paper in mine. I felt absurdly
cheated, positively dragonish, and protested to the waiter. He returned with another plate and two more cookies. This time, I took
both fortunes for my own. (The girl was, by now, utterly silent.)
My first fortune was clear and upbeat: "You will hear encouraging
news"; my second, cloudy, faintly ominous: "Two propositions yet
to come. The darker one is best" . . . I laughed aloud at both messages but couldn't laugh them off. Sheer nonsense, yet for hours
afterward, I found myself puzzling what these words might conceivably mean.

I should add that I wasn't the only embarrassment in that restaurant. Earlier, another diner had shouted rudely at the waiter,
"Tools! I want tools!" He meant regular eating utensils, spoons,
forks, and knives, not chopsticks.

So much for multiculturalism.

So much for social distraction!

I'd learned my lesson: it seemed easier, pleasanter for everyone
involved, to simply give up trying, so I stayed late at the office and
drowned myself in paperwork. Back at the apartment came the
reckoning, though: sitting and stewing for hours, same chair, same

thoughts going round and round. And it didn't improve my mood when, spinning the radio dial on my way to music or weather, I picked up a rebroadcast of one of Rush Limbaugh's rants calling street people "outdoorsmen"—happy campers wearing doleful masks to fool the fools, those bleeding heart liberals who threatened to gobble up the airwaves. Homelessness, according to Rush, was a deliberate, willful, in-your-face lifestyle choice.

Sadly, I was back to smoking again. It helped keep my hands occupied, for one thing. And the visible breath ripples I created were an important part of it, something out there from me in here, a connection, a visible proof that the me-in-here existed. I resisted the impulse to buzz Father Evans, didn't have the strength to dial up the reception desk at St. Joe's, to end the suspense by asking to speak to Michael in person. In some way, I guess, I preferred not to know if, or what, he'd decided.

By then, I was full of misgivings. Doubts. I'd gotten the mother to agree—that part was easy enough—she expected some sort of payoff, I knew. We'd set the time and place. The nagging question remained: would Michael show up? For his usual scheduled appointment at least, if only to let me know that he wouldn't be going along with my plan? And what if he *did* consent to the meeting?

Suppose the delusion I meant to free him from—to cure him of—was all that held Michael's world together?

What then?

There was no one at the office with whom I felt free enough to share these thoughts, so I turned to June as a sounding board. We met at the Greek place on Fourteenth and walked down to the Village afterward, talking all the while.

Had distance and time apart made us wiser to one another? Probably not.

"Sometimes I thought you were playing a game," she said. "Then the game got to be real. Like a man pretending not to hear ending up deaf. Or a man pretending to be mad . . . Hamlet, wasn't it?"

"Hamlet wasn't mad. He was crazy-sane, like a fox."

"Whatever." Old habits never die and we kept feeding each

other fresh provocations as we walked. June knew all the hot buttons. Passing a derelict form stretched out on the pavement, she'd taunt, "Your kind of people."

"That's right," I'd agree calmly, refusing to rise to the bait, "my kind of people."

"It's a kind of reverse snobbery. The way you dress lately. It's pathetic. Just look at you—you're beginning to look more and more like one of them . . ."

This much was true: Even in the early best-behavior days of our going together, we'd be taking some scenic walk and my enjoyment would be spoiled by the sight of two supermarket carts parked out where they didn't belong, loaded with pots, pans, blankets, old boots, crumpled clothing, a rolled-up window shade and spools of wire, a tarp stretched between them for a makeshift roof, a figure hidden, lying or crouching beneath—someone's idea of home. It would be an evening in spring or early fall and June and I strolling along the East River hand in hand and it would be lovely, all five bridges lit up, strutting their jewels, party boats blaring, bright yellow water taxis chugging past . . . At Pier 17, we'd stop for seafood, alongside the old sailing ships, their masts swaying in the currents—and it would be magnificent, simply magnificent.

Yet, all the way coming and going, I never failed to find them. Alerted by faint tappings and rustlings, my gaze would snag every third or fourth bench on the huddled human shapes, half-buried under heaps of clutter.

My *kind of people*.

"It's tantamount to force-feeding," June insisted. "*Your* idea of food. Ram it down his throat, why not?"

Of course—I never expected otherwise—she disapproved of my plans for intervention, all the while insisting that she understood the pressures of time and official protocol, and my sense of urgency.

"But that's all from *your* point of view. Michael's not your project—not your salvage operation. It's *his* life, after all."

"His life to mess up? To lose?"

"His life to whatever. Not up to you."

"It's for his own good."

"So you've said. Twice already."

"If nothing changes, he's finished."

"You mean, if nothing changes *you're* finished with him—*you* lose. And Michael manages to survive as he's somehow managed all his life up until now. Or he doesn't survive. You think he doesn't get it—the hardness of the world? He must have some street-smarts after all this time. But whatever he decides, it's *his* business. It's not like he's the first client you've had to give up on. Win one, lose one, Tom, that's the way the cookie crumbles. So . . . you lose one . . ."

"Just write him off?"

"He's not the first, he's not the only. He's only one. What's the big deal? It's not like there's some super talent going to waste here. And, really—who's this about? Is it Eddie? Is this about your brother? No one ever admitting . . . Your never knowing—"

"It's possible I can offer him a way out. There's a chance."

"Where did I read—did I see it on TV?—about people from upscale neighborhoods dining from Dumpsters? They talked it up as a protest against waste, the latest trend in urban ecology. These people hang around the best restaurants and grocery stores and have regular gatherings and feasts. They're called 'Freegans,' by the way. I bet you can google it. Check it out."

"Michael isn't feasting or gathering—he lives on trash. Trash laced with rat poison."

Was June listening? Traffic was thick and there was too much competing noise. Racing to make a light, our hands brushed by accident. I seized the opportunity and latched on purposefully while we dashed from curb to curb. Meeting no resistance, I made the mistake of pushing it, interweaving my fingers with hers.

Finger by finger, she extricated herself.

June wasn't done with me, though. And she had been listening. "A way out? Are you out of your mind? You're rubbing his face in the dirt. 'Here's your real mother—a horror show—'"

"She isn't a horror show—she's human."

"Horribly human."

"The point is, she's *real*. Isn't it odd for *you*—June-the-Pragmatist, the Realist—to call facing facts 'rubbing his face in the dirt'?" Seemed to me she was contradicting herself, big time. "Would it be better for him to live in a fantasy world forever? Or to die because of it? He's made it through by the skin of his teeth—so far. His luck won't last forever . . . Reality"—and I might have been quoting June herself—"it's not an option."

"You want him to face the real world?" June wasn't letting up. "Real life—don't make me laugh! Get real yourself, Tom! You've meddled all you can."

And I was reduced to sputtering in reply, "Someone ought . . . someone must . . ."

"Someone! How many times do I have to say it? It's his choice, not yours."

There was nothing more for either of us to say, little I hadn't, at some point, argued against myself. It was crazy-eights the way we connected, June and I. Sometimes I wanted to stop her mouth— I'd kiss her just to stop her mouth.

Right then, I wanted desperately to change the subject. We'd reached the foyer of June's building. I stood, a wall paneled with mailboxes in front of me. As she busied herself, rummaging around in her purse for her key, her face drawn down, I studied her ear, the crescent of June's ear, moon-pale against the blackness of her hair.

June has the nicest ears, small and perky, with the tiniest lobes. I couldn't keep my hand from creeping, my finger poised to trace its seashell coil, that lovely twist . . .

"Hey, that tickles!" She swatted my hand away.

"Won't bite," I promised. Right then I wanted nothing more than to nibble. And, moving swiftly, I managed to sneak a kiss. She suffered my kiss; I tasted lip balm—clove, I think; our teeth clashed. "No—no—and no, Tom!" She thumbed my cheek aside. "Don't you ever get the message?"

She didn't invite me up to her apartment but didn't dismiss me at once, either. I stood my ground there in the foyer, staring at the tiles beneath my feet, stalled on a checkerboard of black and gray.

Then she took up our old theme again—it seemed to be our only topic of conversation.

"For cripes sake, Tom," was her parting shot, "get over it! It's a wide world out there. Michael's hardly a speck in the big picture. You're obsessed, you're *stuck*—change the channel!"

24

The Night Before

I couldn't stay put in the apartment that last evening so walked myself down to the Forty-Second Street library. I had an excuse—a
sudden, overpowering need to get my hands on Schreber's memoir—that touchstone of delusional clarity. I had no copy of my own
and hadn't glanced at the book since my student days.

And there, ahead, was the grand stairway and, flanking it, the
lordly lions Patience and Fortitude, watching us go by with the
patience and fortitude only stone knows. Reasonably certain that
the main entrance at the top of the steps would be shut at night,
I pressed on past, turned the corner, and entered by a dim side
door.

Moving through the marble corridors, past the public catalog on
into the main reading room, I was awed as if for the first time. With
its chandeliers and book-lined upper galleries, not to mention the
ornately framed painting of the ceiling itself—rose-tinted clouds
idling in a turquoise sky—Room 315 bore all the resemblance
Versailles might to the world of the street below. I don't mean to
sound ungrateful—on the contrary, it was a marvelous escape and
open to anyone and everyone.

Sitting across from me, sharing a lamp, was a case in point: an
unshaven man in a padded jacket, who kept his hood drawn up.

The place was so jam-packed that I had no choice but to sit facing him. True, it was chilly out, but inside it was sweltering. The man looked like one of my clients—homeless, or on his way to it. And though he didn't seem to be that old, his cheeks flapped and folded as he muttered to himself—he was toothless. Most likely he'd come in off the street hoping to warm up and get off his feet.

He'd amassed a number of books from the open reference shelves and built a small fortification around himself. Staring quietly, intently, but *sightlessly* (I don't know how I knew this) at the volume propped open in front of him, his pose of studious engagement was almost convincing. When he lifted the volume to move it closer to the light, I was amazed to learn that it was an index of global stocks for 1969. Standard & Poor's, no less.

All the while I waited for my book to be fetched from the stacks, he never turned the page.

Then, suddenly, despite the stage-set he'd created (the props carefully arranged to ward off interference), he blew his cover.

"Act-ually," he announced much too loudly, "this table is really nothing!" When he smacked the wood, I wasn't the only one who jumped.

An eerie quiet resumed. I studied the long row on row of bowed heads, gilded by the gold-gleaming lamps. But as soon as Schreber's memoir was brought to me, I forgot everything else. Riffling through its pages, I was on the hunt for signs of what Bleuler called "double-bookkeeping," prevaricating phrases such as "gave the impression," "so-called," "there appeared to be," "so to speak," "up to a point," "in a way," clues to the reader that his delusions, however vivid, were not as real to Schreber as outsiders assumed—present, yes; entirely real, no—and that Schreber had known the difference all along.

Unfortunately, the translator had assumed that such equivocating expressions were unimportant, mere verbal tics, which he'd done his best to eliminate. Still—he'd missed enough of them to fuel my suspicion that Schreber knew that his visions and voices were *mental* happenings, not events in the world. These admissions, once you knew how to look for them, were glaring:

What I directly feel is that the talking voices (lately in particular the voices of the talking birds) as *inner voices* move like long threads into my head . . .

. . . *inner voices* . . . The italics were Schreber's own.

"This lamp isn't really a lamp!" the man across from me broke in. Another page, another revelation:

I did not know whether to take the streets of Leipzig through which I traveled as only theatre props, perhaps in the fashion in which Prince Potemkin is said to have put them up for Empress Catherine II of Russia during her travels through the desolate country so as to give her the impression of a flourishing countryside. At Dresden Station, it is true, I saw a fair number of people who gave the impression of being railway passengers.

. . . gave the impression . . .

"Now—what's *this?*" The man across from me lifted one hand to the lamplight, turning it over slowly with a puzzled expression, as if it were an object dropped from the ceiling which, just that instant, had accidentally landed in his lap. He flexed his long, sickle-shaped thumb.

He smacked the table again. At that, the security guard up front started straight for our table. I tried not to stare as he closed in. This was none of my responsibility, I was off duty, and besides—

"Caref—it'll snap off!" A mistake to tap the man on his shoulder, and quite unnecessary, as it turned out. Once started, the offender shambled along compliantly enough, exchanging pleasantries with the guard—"And how are you doing today?" "Not too bad." "Chilly out there." "Bit nippy, yes."—I could not believe my ears.

It was a relief to know that I had no role to play, the situation resolved without my having to lift a finger.

Quiet resumed, thickened. Until one of the readers coughed, "Ehud!"—a concert cough, dry and circumspect.

Then, "Ihutt!" A head lifted, a hand ruffled a page.

Bending to my task, I read,

> . . . From then on I also gained the impression that Professor Flechsig had secret designs against me; this seemed confirmed when I once asked him . . . whether he honestly believed that I could be cured, and held out certain hopes, but could no longer— at least so it seemed to me—look me straight in the eye . . .

. . . so it seemed to me . . .

Seemed!

I'd found enough to bolster my case—or at least my *hope*—that even the most entrenched delusions were never entirely without openings, if only you knew how to look for them. I bundled up and made my way back into the night.

Out in the street, the chill had intensified. I was surprised to find a young girl standing by the boarded-up newspaper kiosk at the edge of Bryant Park, panhandling. There couldn't have been much profit in it—it was a sorry night to be out.

Yet she was singing. As if for the joy of it. Her voice, high and clear, had an unexpected sweetness. The song was nothing I'd ever heard before and I lingered despite the cold, reluctant to move on, throwing a five into the coffee can at her feet, asking would she mind singing it one more time.

The lyrics, as much as I could make of them, were strange:

> "Oh, do not blame the hen that the rooster died. (This was the refrain.)
> 'Twas the nightingale who called to him
> In the green garden . . ."

No garden here . . . but bleak pavement, refuse blowing, hunched figures scurrying past. Yet the girl's voice shimmered and, rising, seemed to fill the air with brightness. As long as the music lasted, I couldn't help feeling shone-upon.

And, inexplicably, I felt too that perhaps my luck was about to change.

25

Eighteen Inches

Hearing nothing from Michael since our last meeting, I'd gone ahead anyway and finalized arrangements. We were due to meet his mother at a coffee shop I'd located not too far from where she lived. For us, leaving from my office, with four stops on the downtown IRT local, no transfers, I anticipated no logistical difficulties.

I'd been hoping against hope all that interminable week. Whenever I said to myself, *I can't go through with this*, I'd think of what he—Michael—was likely to be going through. That cut my discomfort down to size.

The night before, on my return home from the library, I'd taken a long soak in the tub. I thought it might calm me. And I tried to recall the song I'd stopped for. Something about green gardens—how'd it go? *Try humming*. I did, but my humming, more creaking than singing, bore no resemblance to the girl's voice rising in darkness, the aching sweetness of that voice.

Apart from her voice, the words "green garden," "nightingale," and "rooster" had lost their power to soothe.

I did manage nearly four hours of sleep after the bath, though, and the night went by.

I must admit I was surprised—astounded, more like it—when

Michael actually showed up, arriving on the dot of one (although he had no watch), according to schedule. His hair was wet-combed, sleeked down flat, his face scrubbed, T-shirt and chinos freshly laundered. I interpreted these signs favorably but did my best to tamp down any surge of unearned optimism. This much was true in any case: it wasn't for my benefit that he'd dressed up!

"No point hanging around—might as well get going," I announced, jumping to my feet as soon as he crossed the threshold. I was so fearful of any hesitation on his part, of the slightest delay.

Then I noticed his backpack.

"Why schlep that around? Why not park it here?"

Astonishingly—he consented.

"We'll park it in my closet," I suggested. "Safer that way. We can stop by on the way back and pick it up."

After I'd locked the office door behind us, Michael paused, touching his hand to the knob, as if already regretful that he'd relinquished his pack. I pressed on.

At that moment I was elated beyond caution. Then, the very next moment, filled with foreboding. *Is this really happening?* I kept asking myself. *Don't be too sure. It can't be this easy . . .* Only my doubt was a sure thing.

Still . . . whatever happened, even if the meeting with his mother turned out to be a total bust, I had Michael's knapsack, an anchor, a handle. A token of his trust, at last.

It was chilly out. Twitchy, brisk crosscutting winds. An afternoon of scuttling clouds, the light touch-and-go, sudden dims and brights, it matched my mood. One minute, I knew our venture was doomed; the next, I couldn't help but feel that Nature was smiling on us, blessing us on our way. Michael was keeping perfect time with me—our steps matched for one entire block.

I tried to caution myself: *So far so good. So far . . . Pacing is all. Not far to go now . . . Only a few more steps . . .*

Walking side by side then, we were, I estimate, about a foot and a half apart. Where was it that I read that eighteen inches was the magic formula—how did they put it?—the optimal distance, the right proportion of push to pull for getting along with others in New York? Any closer and we'd implode like locusts; farther—we'd fly apart, scatter like grains of sand before the wind, mere bleeping particles, receding ever faster, fainter . . .

There were few people about. A runaway shopping cart rattled down the street, crashing at the curb, spilling groceries as it went over. Seconds later, a hooded figure dashed out of a doorway to claim the spoils, which must have been a windfall for him. Michael seemed not to notice any of this, he was still keeping step with me, but his motions struck me as robotic and he kept his eyes on his feet.

Better slow down!

I'd just as soon turn around and go back—out of the blue came this crazy thought. *While there's still time. What's done can be undone* . . . And yet there I was, moving relentlessly forward. As if I could outrun what I must have known all along: this would have no good ending.

After we crossed the street, Michael seemed to be dragging a little; even in low gear, I was consistently getting a half-step ahead of him. So I forced myself to creep along, fearful all the while that I was giving him too much time to think, to reconsider. What's more, I realized that, with each lagging step, *I* was losing faith in this entire venture.

We walked in silence . . . *A companionable silence,* I tried to tell myself.

Almost there. Only a few more . . . I could read the finer print on the IRT sign coming up. The slower our pace, the faster my thoughts raced. What if he took one glance at his mother and split? What if he decided that she was an impostor?

I wondered, too: What if she decided that *he* was the impostor? What if she decided not to show up? But a no-show from the mother I could handle, I imagined. After all, Michael had lived all these years with her absence; he'd garlanded the empty place until no longer empty, so thickly tangled with hearts and flowers.

I remarked on the weather. He murmured something I didn't catch. Then we started down into the subway. At the bottom of the stairs, I turned to pass him a token—

"Penny for your thoughts," I said.

No reply.

No one there! I pivoted—*no one!*—where could he go? I had no idea where I'd lost him. It couldn't be far back, though. At the turnstile? Middle of the stairs? He'd been with me, our steps almost matched, his starting to drag as we went on, but no more than a half-step as I adjusted to his pace. Did he lose his nerve at the last moment?

But maybe he'd surged on ahead of me—it wasn't out of the question. I pushed through the turnstile, then, reminding myself how unlikely it was that he'd go forward on his own, doubled back on the route we'd taken. I want to say that I raced back to the office, but it couldn't have been that fast, each step a sinking.

And then, only then, did it register, the last thing he'd said:

"I know where I am."

Back at the office: not a trace.

As if he'd evaporated into thin air! As if I'd only dreamed him into being!

26

Parts of a World

He'll come back for the knapsack soon enough, is what I kept telling myself. My obligation right then was to the mother, so, for a second time that afternoon, I set out to meet her. I still might manage to arrive only fifteen minutes or so late.

Would she wait? I had a hunch she would.

And there she was. Only a few of the tables were occupied, people stuffing their faces, staring at nothing. She was seated by a window at a table for four near the door. I paused before blundering inside into I-knew-not-what. It was clear that she, too, had made a special effort and groomed herself with care for a special occasion: red dress, red button earrings, makeup—a rosy dab on each cheek—and, of all things, she'd curled her hair! It formed a nimbus of bright bubbles around her face. The total effect was clownish.

She was all too obviously stalling for time, with one hand, warming her fingers around a steaming cup, the other, stirring and stirring with beggarly calm persistence, tracing circles with her spoon.

Then she glanced up and I saw (but how could I at that distance?) something gleaming, tears perhaps, eyes bright with what might be tears, or a trick reflection maybe, flicker of light and shadow, or blisters in the glass, or condensation from the warmth inside the room, the window sweating . . . No mistaking the hand stretched out to me, though, it hung, afloat in midair, half in greeting, half withheld—uncertain. And . . . I still can't make sense of it. If she'd been sure, if she'd given a clear wave in recognition, if she'd tapped or merely brushed the pane with her fingertips, there'd have been no way out. If I'd taken only one more step toward the door . . . But I wavered, she wavered, there was only that blur of hazy motion.

I turned, fled, never looked back—

The damage was done; there could be no appeal. No excuse. For what I did. What I failed to do. For not even *trying* to explain. But what words could ever make this right?

What *had* I been thinking? The options were never there. Truth was, I didn't think, didn't imagine, beyond the (salutary, I hoped) shock of recognition. For Michael's mother, I'd assumed that the impact would be negligible. Convenient to assume so—it showed how little I cared. For Michael, I knew the impact would be profound. I fully intended to kick the anchor out from under him. (The anchor that wasn't there.) It had been a risk, but a calculated risk—I've gone over and over this—he could not continue as he had. Amend that: *we* could not continue.

So much for Michael, his dream in tatters.

There are decisions we make that we don't come back from. I'd made no attempt to contact the mother since that day, and she would have had no way of getting in touch with me. What could I say? She'd never asked for my name, so she had no handle—and no credibility, anyway—for complaint. She'd been an instrument, part of a plan, and the plan fell through. Yes, my professionalism had been badly compromised, yet, harried as we were in the office, no one seemed to notice.

Or maybe someone had noticed—*something*; the latest personnel changes certainly gave me pause. Karina's promotion, for one thing, and—this came as a surprise—it would be Martin who'd take her place. Not everyone was happy about this. Two of the black staffers made no secret of feeling miffed—Martin is lily white. They had a point: it was time for a person of color. Then again, going by seniority, I should have been next in line. But, no,

164

it was Martin-the-calm-and-collected, the man who bowed to his veggie burger. (*And to his clients?* I wondered.) We could use some calm and respect around the office, so maybe it would be for the best. I never really coveted a supervisor's job, anyway—too many headaches, too much paper to push. Karina would be transferring to the downtown office soon. I wish her all the best, I do.

It's so hard for me to concentrate these days.

I'd do better in future (I'd made up my mind to), investing less, caring less. It's only a job, what I do, no longer a mission. I'd make sure to follow procedures from here on out. With one minor exception: Still stalling for time, I resisted the SPMI—the seriously and persistently mentally ill—label, placing Michael's folder under Status Change, a holding category. Weeks later, following the prescribed sequence, I was obliged to transfer his case folder to Inactive. In due course, his name would be shifted to the Dead File or simply lost to all files, among the legions of the Disappeared. So many names, recorded or lost . . . it's hard to appreciate: they were all people once . . . My few efforts at tracking—hospitals, morgues— have revealed nothing, ending with what I already know: my own reports. It's almost impossible to trace a person who's determined to get lost.

Weeks and months have gone by, the seasons moving through the usual. I, alone, seemed to be dragging.

There is no steadiness in me.

I arranged to have a talk with Father Evans. Face-to-face, for a change.

There was some commotion at St. Joe's when I entered the day-room. A number of residents were clustered around a small Christmas tree they'd been decorating with strings of popcorn and cut-out paper snowflakes. They'd been arguing whether the tinfoil star on top leaned to the left or the right and roped me into the fray. "To the right," I judged, then, unsure, added my usual caveat: "But, really, it all depends on the angle of the viewer." They decided it was leaning to the left.

"Anybody hear anything from Michael?" No harm in asking, I

figured. "Michael who?" was the only answer I got—from a young man whose name also happened to be Michael. The turnover must be swift at St. Joe's; not one of them could recall an earlier Michael.

I scanned the bulletin boards anyway, hoping to discover a lost-and-found list and perhaps a mention of something Michael might have left behind, but found only the standard season's greetings on crude, hand-crayoned scenes of shepherds and starlight and smiling snowmen. There was a list of house rules—RULES FOR GETTING ALONG—exactly what you'd expect: if you turned it on, turn it off . . . if you moved it, put it back . . . if you value it, keep your eye on it . . . if it belongs to someone else, ask . . . if you don't know how to operate it, keep your hands off . . .

Father Evans welcomed me into his office and offered me something to drink. I assured him I had no intention of staying that long. I had to say that I wasn't entirely clear on why I'd come. Of course, I was being disingenuous—counting on my disclaimer, its blatant untruthfulness, to start things off.

The place was a mess: blistered walls, files heaped on the orthopedic chair in a corner, old black shoes with hammertoe bulges on the floor alongside it. An ancient electric typewriter on a stand—no sign of a computer. As for his desk, it was easy to see where he'd been taking his meals. I spoke the obvious: "Guess you're pretty busy. Looks like you're working on grants . . ."

He nodded and sighed. "Polishing my begging bowl. Trying to survive on less and less . . . Well, you know as well as I do. The money's drying up."

"If it's not a good time . . ."

"Don't know when there'll be a better," he was quick to reply. But the interruptions, the complaints, were constant; Father Evans was continually going and coming, padding around in his sock feet to arbitrate. So-and-so was playing his music too loud—not everybody liked rap. So-and-so had hogged the snack food supposed to be shared by all . . . had plugged up the toilet . . . must be jerking off in the shower, he was taking so much time . . .

The priest would return and resettle, raising his eyebrows and smiling, his only comment.

"Just wondering," I was curious, "how you handle all that . . ."

Father Evans shrugged. "We didn't fall out of trees, you know. I've got my feet on the ground—I've been around. Seen pretty much everything by now. So—where were we?"

We weren't getting anywhere until his night-shift assistant came on board, freeing the priest to shut his door and give more thought to what he was saying. As best I can recall, here's the gist of it:

"You want to know what faith is . . . Personally, I don't think it has much to do with weeping statues. It's not a thunderbolt. It isn't *knowing*. It isn't even belief—too often, a head trip. Faith and belief . . . people tend to think they're the same thing . . .

"All that talk about a 'leap of faith' . . . No leap for me. It's nothing at all like flying. Slogging, maybe—more like it . . ." He smiled but I could tell he was serious.

Our conversation was full of stops and starts. He stared at his hand in silence for a moment then took up the theme again: "Faith is the opposite of certainty, I think. Stumbling through darkness as though it were light. Only—once in a great while, well, maybe a glimmer of . . . Better not quote me on this," he added. "It's not exactly the Party line."

He started to mumble then. He seemed to be negotiating something with himself. Problem was, he'd dropped his voice and the television in the common room was going full blast; there was a laugh track running. By the time someone stepped in and turned the volume down, we'd lost the thread of what had gone before. Father Evans's mood seemed to have shifted.

After that came the part I can't figure but can't get out of my head. "There's this story," he said, "keep meaning to check it out. If ever I find the time. I've no idea whether it's true. Probably just another one of those stories, so better not quote me on this, either. I'm sure to have scrambled the details—time, place. Other things. It bears on your question, I think, or why else would it come to mind now? Anyway—for what it's worth. It's about the

Jews in the ghettos at the time of their so-called emancipation. As I understand it, Napoleon ordered a gathering of rabbis and scholars, called it a 'Sanhedrin,' though there'd been no such thing for more than a thousand years. The Jews were given an offer—an end to their exile, an open door out into the world beyond the ghetto walls, but only on condition that they give up waiting for the Messiah." He paused again.

"I'm interested," I said. "What happened?"

"What you might expect. Some opted for the world—for assimilation. Some stayed within walls and refused to budge, choosing to wait and hold fast, refusing to be dispossessed of their ancient hope. Which was the better course, do you think?"

"Those who broke free. Obviously."

"You think? Take a look at the history, though. Those who left did do better—for a while. But only for a while . . . Over the long run? Not really, not so different. And, as everybody knows, the Messiah failed to show up. So what's the moral? That the world keeps no promises? That faith is no guarantee? That faith outlives belief?"

Abruptly he turned on himself. "But where were we? I've forgotten your question."

He'd been loosening up, unbuttoning, in more ways than one. While talking, he'd unfastened his top shirt button, drawing out a strip of white plastic, the dog collar part, and tossing it unceremoniously into a coffee jar filled with writing utensils. "What are you *really* asking?" He leaned forward, his fingers trailing over a patch of skin he'd missed when shaving. With his pug-face, his nose sort of mashed in, and his powerfully hinged jaws, he was not a handsome man. I wondered whether he'd boxed in his youth or had been born that way. "This is all about your client, isn't it?" he asked. "Not letting you go, is he?" The man seemed perfectly capable of carrying on both sides of our conversation solo. "Mustn't blame yourself," he added. "You did what you could."

I hadn't come for confession, I broke in; it was important to brook no confusion on this.

Father Evans's gaze grew searching, a spotlight; I felt it, I felt murky, far from clear. "About Michael, yes . . . your client . . . I know you're worried. Not without reason. But maybe the world will be gentle with him this time."

"Gentle! The world will eat him alive."

"You did what you could," he said again, and then, as was his habit, his peculiar way of concentrating, Father Evans closed his eyes and went on talking. "I tried, too." He sounded weary or wistful. "But let's not kid ourselves—none of it amounted to much. Try looking at it his way. Our feeding left him famished; the food he scavenged for filled him. What better had you to offer?"

"Better than moldy, who-knows-how-old bread? Almost anything!" I was sure of it.

Father Evans spread his palms. "Stale, moldy bread transformed by—what? Hunger? Delusion? Hope against hope? . . . Dare I say love?" and his eyes remained closed as he waved his hands over a desk spotted with crumbs.

Nan kept calling, inviting me out to L.A. for Christmas. Christmas! So many months away . . . What were my plans? Too far off. I had no plans. I couldn't leave the city for the foreseeable future. Impossible to explain: why I *must* stay.

Months passed and Michael did not show up. Not even a footprint. I kept telling myself that he'd scrape by—fed by God's ravens, who knows, managing somehow to keep on keeping on— that he was alive. He was alive or he wasn't. Not in my power to make it one or the other . . .

So there I was, left (literally) holding the bag. His backpack sat where he left it in my office closet, in my keeping. I never saw Michael separate from his pack before, that's why I couldn't help thinking he'd show up again, if only to reclaim it and be on his way. I ransacked the thing for any clue as to what he might be up to, where he might hang out.

There was a purse inside full of unidentified pills. Were these a backlog or meant for the month ahead? Had he been squirreling away his pills at St. Joe's, rarely taking them? For how long? I called Dr. Kirsch but there was little he could do. He reminded me that, without medication, Michael could expect nothing but a repeat of his old cycle. A cycle all too familiar: picked up by the police and hospitalized again or poisoned or beaten to a pulp by young toughs prowling their turf—but there was no need to spell it out.

For all his scrounging, there was only one item I'd have counted worth saving from the crusher: a cut glass doorknob. Very nice, actually, it looked like crystal. The rest of his pickings were pretty pathetic: a bunch of plastic utensils and paper napkins; a torn sweatshirt with its Department of Sanitation—*NYDS*—logo intact; a garbage collection schedule for odd- and even-numbered streets; two lawn and leaf bags; a neatly folded square of tarp; clean boxers and a pair of sweat socks; an ancient, obsolete office pad I used for scratch paper, lifted from my desk. A much-handled black-and-white photo of a family (mom, dad, two kids, one of each kind, a wedge of bright beach behind them). I stared and stared, trying to discover why he'd bother to keep this. The setup was generic, the people also: four of them standing in a row, squinting at the sun. Turning the thing over, I found only the year "1992" penciled on the back, not a clue as to place or people and, anyway, no resemblance to Michael or his mother, so I suspect he simply borrowed a family, someone else's life. Almost missed, hidden away in an old sock in the bottom corner of the bag, I uncovered a child's toy, this tiny matchbox model car—a silvery Nissan in mint condition, complete with side-view mirrors, door handles, and brake lights—clearly a prized item. Something else at the bottom, deep down: a small spiral notebook, with a few serrated ribbons of torn pages still clinging. Was *this* what he meant to unearth when he opened his knapsack to show me something during his last office visit—when I cut him off?

Numbers penciled in everywhere. Scavenging tallies, I assumed —intake, outtake . . . earnings and expenses. Many of the numbers, I noticed, were multiples of five—most likely he'd been collecting bottles and cans for a nickel apiece. But all of that told me precious little new. There was a page which I brooded over:

found a new place

A list of finds—"gifts" in his reckoning (I suppose):

happy meal toy gone—banana—pizza almost half . . . 16 pennies . . .

Clearly, he had his own world, a neat little ecosystem of sorts.
Then I came along and—*What's this?*

always = in all ways

Last entry, a page by itself, the letters shaky:

it must be so

27

Desperate Measures

I couldn't shake the feeling that he was nearby, hidden in plain sight.

I sketched, as best I could, a portrait of Michael and brought it out each time I visited one of the nonofficial recycling centers I'd found in the phone book. Manhattan Metals . . . Borough-Wide Bottle . . . Integrated Waste . . . Afterlife Industries . . . Wranglers . . . Beautiful Savior Redemption . . . Agave Associates. To name a few.

I'd had no idea there were so many.

I sorted the list neighborhood by neighborhood and must have checked out a full dozen before coming to the conclusion that I was getting nowhere.

My reception was standard in every outfit but one: the person at the intake counter would either shrug and say nothing or, ". . . Can't help you there."

Only the man in the front booth at Pentheus Processing was willing to give me the time of day. He smiled wanly behind two panes of bulletproof glass. There followed an intricate dance of fingers through a slot meant for money transactions: I lifted the lid on my side, nudged the sketch forward, and shut the lid before he would consent to raise the lid inside, draw the paper to him, lower the lid, and start to look it over.

There was a long pause.

"Well . . ." he pronounced finally—hardly worth the hassle. He spoke through a microphone. Even so, I had to strain to hear him over the screech of shredding metal.

"You want to know what sort of clientele I deal with?" he said.

I said I'd be interested.

"You'd be surprised. Some of them look pretty well off. Nice cars, designer clothes—go figure! But the others . . . most of them . . . off the street. The usual suspects."

Again, he bent to my sketch. "Looks like one of those police drawings. You know? The kind they mash together in a computer using reports from so-called witnesses."

"You're not undercover, are you?"—this last question only half-serious, for he answered himself right away: "'Course not. And, of course, you wouldn't tell me if you were.

"Well, anyway, I haven't seen him. I don't think so—no. Problem is, see, nothing stands out. This man in the picture here, he could be anyone—you, me, anybody . . ."

There were new developments on the Dumpster scene, I'd noticed, none of them good. In the upscale neighborhoods, behind the tonier shops, some of the lids were sprouting locks. And many of the newer bins were eight feet tall, which meant you had to (literally) dive in or use one of those grappling hooks on a long pole to fish things out. So the better items had to be scarcer than ever these days.

How did I know this? I—I must admit—had been scouting. I even—but only twice, two separate bins, both in the immediate vicinity of my office—I had, yes, made drop-offs. In one: a cheeseburger with all the trimmings, double-bagged in plastic, and a small bottle of vitamins. In another: a carton of fried chicken and a thick slab of chocolate, the kind they call bittersweet, not milky—I remembered him saying he didn't care for milky.

It's still hard to believe I actually did this. I mean, made the drop-offs, mapped them out beforehand, surveyed the sites that looked promising, then circled back to my selected target, all the while glancing nervously over my shoulder, trying to avoid the staring eyes of respectable people passing in the street.

I slinked around. I could have done my business under cover of darkness and avoided this embarrassment but figured that would be guaranteed useless since the collection trucks came round early in the morning. Instead, I made my deposits at midday, so the things wouldn't be carted away immediately yet wouldn't land at the bottom of the bin, too far down for Michael to be able to reach them. And, yes, I'd devoted more time than I care to admit to thinking through each least detail.

So many calculations . . .

Slipping out of the office at the noon hour, carrying what looked like my lunch bag, I moved furtively in full light. I knew (in my right mind) how inconspicuous I must have been yet felt my face mottle with shame, my intention incandescent for all to see.

My first deposit was utterly wasted. I'd tossed in my offering and was about to let down the lid when I noticed an old man crouching behind the bin. He looked pretty derelict—and guilty—and with reason, having knifed the bottom out of a bulging plastic bag. There were beer cans scattered around him, a torn pizza box, a spatter of pennies, bloodied menstrual pads, chicken bones, condoms, rotted fruit, and, surrounding the debris, what at first looked like grains of rice—maggots swarming! The old man startled when he saw me and spewed. Obscenities drizzled from his lips.

Out of that alley I flew—

And nearly collided with a taxi cruising down the street. I tottered on the curb, catching my breath, and stared in amazement as a yuppie couple in helmets, knee and wrist guards Rollerbladed by; perfectly ordinary, yet it struck me as the strangest sight in the world. Clearly, I needed to stay away from Dumpsters in the future.

I couldn't stick to my resolve, though. *Only one last try*, I promised myself.

So I made a second foray, and it was the last.

I know how pathetic this sounds. How wasteful. Throwing perfectly good food into the trash ought to be a crime. Anybody watching me would think I was crazy. It *was* crazy. The gesture was wildly extravagant and, at the same time, paltry, meager, my offering next to nothing. A mere drop in the bucket. As I vaulted my packet over the rim of the Dumpster, I worried about placement (how visible, accessible, etc.), but I wasn't prepared to make any readjustment if it failed to land properly. And I had all I could do to keep myself from tossing in a note as well, detailing for whom the packet was meant and reminding whoever retrieved it (someone who knew someone who might have heard something?) that I was holding Michael's backpack, waiting for him to reclaim it. Only the echo of Michael's own words "mercy bucket!" called to mind as I banged down the lid with a loud metallic clatter—a taunt, as I now heard it—brought this madness to a halt.

28

City of Salt

All that was solid seemed to dissolve, to melt before my eyes.

The World Trade Towers were falling—pillars of salt, crumbling to salt. Between bites, I watched them fall. They weren't birds, those darker grains which flecked from the windows and, for an instant, floated, seemed to take flight . . . One, two, three heartbeats, I paused, spoon in the air . . . then resumed, raising the spoon to my lips, swilled, and swallowed.

Still at it . . . A week had passed and it was the same loop of television footage going round in endless reprise. The same innocent amazement: a day so lovely it was impossible to believe in death, a sky so blue it stung. I shifted to radio but it was no better. There was new theme music, at least, but it, too, was thick and somber. Music that would bludgeon me to my knees if I let it. Music that hammered, *This is what you must feel.* So many missing, so many dead, and *so near*—I couldn't wrap my mind around it; I didn't know what I felt. Was I a monster? Was I alone in this?

Some said we were in recovery then; some said we'd never recover. Different, or the same? I'm still trying to sort it out. *Both,* I thought, *a mix* . . . Yet the differences came to mind first. Small ones—like drinking more bottled water than before, water from the Ozarks or upstate, water from anywhere else, trusting nothing from our own taps. Trivial, but a fact.

Down in the subway and out on the streets, no question, civility had increased. At the corner of Sixty-Third and Columbus, a man, letting himself down carefully onto the curb, started vomiting, quietly and politely, into his hat. A passerby hollered over to him, "You all right?" but the retching man waved him on his way. A woman knelt alongside him, right there at the curb, offering her handkerchief to wipe his mouth. The man did not refuse. That was not an isolated happening, either; there'd been a whole slew of random acts of kindness. Hard to imagine anything like this in "normal" times. Or to recall people stopping, right in the midst of things, just to weep. Perhaps there were always incidents like these, but we were too busy to notice before.

Grief counseling offices were springing up everywhere—competition, but it didn't interfere with our outfit; there was more than enough sorrow to go around. Misfortune has always been our currency, nothing new there. There were a few operational changes, though. A front door screener who meant business, for one thing. (Gary's toy gun prank would never pass.) And we'd been fire-inspected, going through the motions of two emergency drills, the entire building evacuated each time. Some of our number used these occasions to extend their lunch breaks. Most milled and clustered, killing time. The mood was surprisingly far from somber, an out-of-school feeling.

McNemeny often came to mind. I wondered how he was faring. I was curious about the rest of his dream, after he saw the bridges burning. He was onto something, but we never let him finish. We refused to see. What was it we never allowed him to say?

I kept asking myself, *But has anything really changed?* Could I put my finger on it?

Tempo, I guess . . . We moved more slowly those days, survivors all, unsure of our steps, as if wading through ash which might be still smoldering. I could have found my way to the site with eyes closed. The very air was toxic: dust of mortar, dust of stone, asbestos, petrochemicals, industrial waste, and (was I imagining this?)

something else, primeval—a faint, fecund rottenness—the scent of death abounding. Pictures of the missing were posted on every lamppost, shop front, plastered on mailboxes, walls, faces smiling out of another life already beyond recall. I brooded over the missing for whom no photographs existed, dim shadow figures, missing before and never noticed (this much was the same), lost forever now.

Some spoke of the place of destruction as "hallowed ground." What could it mean—this hallowing? Some sort of force-field surrounding the rubble, gilding, canceling death? Were they flocks of angels, those torrents of white paper (filled with numbers) raining down from on high? On Fulton Street, walking toward Liberty, I found scraps still ungathered, stirring restlessly in the slightest gust of wind. I saved one, a photocopied listing of mutual funds and futures, revealing at one edge the impress of the hand holding the paper down. It haunts me, that ghost hand, the curve of the lifeline between thumb and wrist so sharply etched.

Religion, too, was in the air. Nuns with charity baskets were camping out on stools in front of the Port Authority subway entrance at Forty-Second Street. Old-fashioned nuns in their old-fashioned penguin costumes, their baskets overflowing. Outside, not far from the Eighth Avenue exit, someone chalked on the pavement, WE RISE UP ANGRY AND FULL OF LOVE! I saw verses from the book of Revelation scribbled on walls. For some, the end of the world was at hand. The end-timers had been waiting for such an event. They trotted out the most amazing coincidences: 9/11 was a distress call, the Lord was trying to signal us, trying to get through. The number 11 kept cropping up. Flight 11 was the first to strike the tower; New York was the eleventh state to join the Union; the twin towers formed a gigantic figure 11 against the sky. Events were foretold, the warnings could not have been clearer. Too many people who should have known better failed to read the signs of the times. Too many still refused to see . . .

End of the world or no, Michael remained as much as ever in my thoughts. I closed my eyes and there he was, standing right in front of me; I opened them and he was invisible but lurking. During our infrequent phone conversations, June continued to probe: How could I persist in mourning one person when so many were lost? She called it an "abstraction deficit." Call it what you like, my small grief unswallowed; if I did not feel for one, I could not feel for any.

There was once a city underneath this city. I pictured the catacombs under the towers, the tunnels, galleries, alcoves, caverns, the once-teeming life in the levels below—zero, subzero, sub-sub, a spider's palace replete with sewer rats, rag-pickers, and the legions of cockroaches who shall inherit this all. Michael wrote, "found a new place"—it might have been there. For all I knew, this might have been one of his old places. He could be anywhere, really. Greyhound bus. Side of the road in Illinois waiting for a hitch, thumb in the air—I knew nothing.

After much backing and forthing, I gave in and bought a small aquarium. My thinking was this: *Calm, it should be calming.* (Why else make them a fixture in psychiatrists' waiting rooms?) As it turned out, though, the tiny neon tetra were bright, agitated flecks, anything but calm. The goldfish were all right; they moved slowly and liked to play hide-and-seek in the toy shipwreck I bought them. I fashioned quite a little world down there at the bottom of the tank: fake coral, fake snails. A ceramic castle around it; strands of ribbon weed spiraled upward toward the light.

I did my best not to overfeed. And only the best of fare: Great Gills Goldfish Nibbles and 5-Flake Frenzy. If not always pacifying, the fish brought movement and color—some semblance of life— into my life. I studied their smooth, slippery forms (no arms, no entanglements), drifting wherever the spirit moved them; I tried to let go of the phantasms of the day.

But the incessant burbling from the tank, the continual flurry of bubbles, also got on my nerves sometimes. The tetra shimmered and flashed as they veered, moving always in packs. The goldfish were more solitary. They drifted past one by one, always staring. I never caught them sleeping. Or maybe they slept with their eyes open; maybe that's what they were doing whenever one of them bumped the glass. Sometimes, when they'd been much too still, I'd go over to them and tap and enjoy the stir I caused. The aquarium was a calculated distraction, but it rarely worked for long. If I moved through my waking hours without giving much thought to Michael, then my dreams spoke of him.

Like this one:

I'm stepping out the back door of the supermarket, leaving the few remaining bananas—mostly green or bruised—inside. The dream says nothing about standing in line, nothing about having to pay. Out on the street I sing out happily to the air, to no one in particular, "I'm bringing the groceries home!" I'm clutching an empty sack. There's a boy in white overalls moving along a window ledge high up on the building in front of me. I'm yelling, "Don't jump! Get back inside!"

He jumps—but it's me who's falling—

Or this: The phone's ringing; it doesn't stop. I race, stumbling over my own feet to catch it in the nick of time. It's long distance, a collect call, the operator asking, "Will you accept this call?" I answer with a shout, "I accept!" and wake with a jolt, not knowing who it was trying to get through, but it's only my alarm that's ringing.

I've been getting a lot of calls lately, though none collect. Ever since 9/11, Nan hasn't let up. She thinks of New York City as a combat zone; it's high time to move to L.A. And June continues to call from week to week. "Just checking. Taking a census is all," she says.

Everyone so concerned.

Our nation is at war, so we've been told. New York City remains a prime target. Constant surveillance of electronic chatter, data streams swirling the globe, yet the mastermind of this havoc, Osama Bin Laden, eludes our latest high-tech intelligence, safe and snug in some primeval cave, dreaming . . . what? We wait to find out. Maybe the stones know but they do not speak to us.

I try not to think of the hijackers who called an inferno "Paradise." They, too, were believers.

❖

"Nice young man," Mr. Morgen said, folding up his glasses and tilting his chair way back. "What else can I say? I've got no complaints—except for his leaving so sudden. Without notice, you understand."

Si Morgen, Michael's last employer, ran an independent manufacturing outfit. What to call it? His business—novelty electronics, assembling miniature racing cars, pen lights, and micro-voice recorders for keychain pendants—was smaller than what you'd normally think of as a factory, but larger than a workshop.

"He was punctual, tidy. Polite enough when spoken to—quiet otherwise. Pretty much kept to himself. He went out somewheres private for lunch so missed whatever the social here. Why do you ask?" He reached for his glasses again. "You family?"

I explained to him in the sketchiest terms my relationship to Michael and mentioned that I'd run into his sort of behavior before: right when the client is on the verge of breakthrough, he bolts and runs.

"Let me show you his unit," Mr. Morgen offered. I followed him out to a small, windowless but brightly lit room where six employees perched on stools fronting a long bench. They were poking minute metal parts with tweezers and what looked like dental probes then passing them up the line. Judging from the rhythmic way their heads moved and the tiny earbuds they all wore, all six were listening to music, each on his own portable recorder, each nodding to a different tempo. Two of them glanced up as we passed, but the others took no notice.

"Gone missing . . . that's too bad," Mr. Morgen reflected, escorting me down the hallway. "Here we are, back where you started." We halted at the door that opened onto the lobby. The sunlight, coming through panels of smoked glass, was clouded; my errand had brought no clarity.

"I can't say I'm all that surprised," he added. "Employees come and go. I'd like to help you out," he said, "if you could tell me exactly what you're looking for. What you need to know. Because,

182

see, Michael wasn't the type to tell anyone his business. He made no waves at all, and one morning he failed to show—never called in sick, or anything—and after that he was gone. Never asked for his paycheck. And he had money owing to him—beats me!" He turned to wave to someone at the other end of the corridor. "I can't think of anything else to say about him, really. If you could tell me what exactly you're looking for . . . Is there something special you need to know? Something I can zero in on?"

I've tried the obvious places. At Grand Central Terminal, I scoped out the malingerers among the bench-sitters, those lurking behind pillars, waiting for things to quiet down, the empty places to reveal themselves. I witnessed the ceremonials of arrival and departure, all too aware that I never said good-bye to Michael, which means I'll never be done with him.

There, and at the Port Authority Terminal on Forty-Second Street, the transit police have been out in full force, rounding up loiterers. Jerry-built booths everywhere soliciting blood donations, plasma donations. I saw right away how useless it was. Too many people, too many gates.

Still . . . I search for him. I keep my pockets full of quarters. One of the panhandlers I pass might know something or know someone who knows. "He was about *so* tall . . ." I'll start, my hand leveling at my eyebrows, before I'm reminded once again of how unremarkable he could seem to other people, how hard it is to pin him down.

When I need to stop and rest, it's usually one of those narrow islands between uptown and downtown lanes on upper Broadway. I pick out a bench, preferably empty. I wait. I think I know why old people so often sit here. As traffic swirls past going and coming, I feel the wind of passage on my face, I know I'm alive.

I'm still here.

The hours drag on. Sometimes in the dead of night I wonder who my neighbor is.

After two, the chill intensifies. It's too cold to get up and fetch another blanket, too cold to sleep without it, so I do not sleep.

Daylight seems another country, morning yet so far away. I try not to think of life out on the street.

Around three, throwing a blanket around me like a cape, I wander the apartment, pace, surf the channels, hoping to stumble again on that church where the deaf were singing. But no, no luck—it was only that one time, it seems, and only a glimpse of their palms rising and falling, fingers flickering like candle flames, silence offered up with such tenderness (as I think back on it now); I still can't forget, can't wrap my mind around the strangeness.

I do find a church, a rebroadcast, but it couldn't be more different: big sound, busy mouths. A young man with a hair arrangement is the pastor. He's a veritable angel of light, wearing a suit so shiny it looks like glass. As he preaches, he drums on the pulpit. "Some people have to go to prison (rat-tat!) to get their attention. Some people have to die (rat-tat-tat!)."

One click is all it takes—

Nothing is too far-out, apparently, for airing at this hour. "For us, in our day, violence and terror are as close as we can come to the Sublime," a long-haired pundit opines. He pushes his wire specs higher up on his nose and gazes bleakly into the camera.

Well, whatever. I suppose he has a point. Nothing distracts me for long. I aim the clicker, and press, and—hey, presto!—it's "Elvis Himselvis!" Click: it's eyebuds on long dancing stalks, ad for some energizing vitamin supplement. Click again: it's a call-in show: dweebs and ditto heads and assorted angries. Then—an old lady who can't sleep for worry. A photograph of her pet parakeet is flashed on the screen, the camera zooms in: the bird is pretty, yes. "That's when he was well," she explains, "and such a comfort to me." Now, she tells us, Sinbad is plucking out all his feathers. The caller weeps. She doesn't know what she's done to offend her pet or how to make her apology known.

Click, click, click . . . An ad for dyspepsia, for joint ache, for credit relief. And always, always, the same reprise—the towers falling. Burning.

Get real, Tom. This is the real world. Get a life—it's not too late.

184

I tell myself all the sensible things. I shelve the remote finally but return to sit facing the television. I stare at the blank screen.

I remind myself that I did the best I could, that I had to act— do something. How impoverished Michael's life was. How unreal. Loveless. How it wasn't a life—

But is this true?

The truth is, Michael wanted nothing from me, or any of us who tried to help; we had no handle to pull him back. He held fast to one thing, *always—in all ways*, even if it turned out to be only a dream. The rest of us merely drift from one bright phantom to the next. I can't help feeling how stingy, scattered, and pale our loves are next to his, how piddling.

Morning comes at last . . . Light chalks the facing wall. Since yesterday we've been expecting the first snow of the season. When I finally fell asleep again (sitting in a hard chair, facing a blank television screen), I dreamed of making my way over drifts of snow holding on to an egg beater, an egg beater with a long handle. I must have been thinking of a ski pole, forgetting the name for it and so fumbling the image, as well.

The radiator sputters and coughs, the bedroom's overheated— so why did I dream about being out in the snow? I wake with a sleep-soured mouth and eyes so dry I have to use my fingers to pry the lids apart.

Tipping the shade, I peer out from my window perch. Pigeons are scavenging on the tar paper of a low-lying roof; someone must have left crumbs for them. A hooded man or woman—so layered there's no telling—creeps out of a shop entry and lurches over to a parking meter on the curb, where he (or she), struggling for the upright, seems to be holding on for dear life. Smoke streams from the subway gratings, rises like incense from the sewer wells. The lights of the street begin their slow dissolve into daylight. It will be a day of bright, bitter cold.

It's time. Little past top of the hour.

"It's 7:06 on Monday morning in the greatest city in the world." I fiddle the radio dial. "Only sixteen shopping days until Christmas."

Must have missed the headline news. You have to wait till half-past or top of the hour for anything serious.

I'm busy setting up the coffee maker, only half-listening, when the emcee (desperate, I guess, to fill a dead-air minute) comes up with the Salvation Army's instructions to their legions of Santas: "Do not hide your chimney. Never have alcohol on your breath . . ."

An internal memo, not meant for public consumption, I'm willing to bet, and it's quickly obliterated by the weather forecast: Lows in the single digits. Wind chill hovering around minus . . . "Bundle up if you have to go out. Stay indoors if you can." They'll be rounding up anyone caught sleeping out on the street to take them to the shelters tonight. I take mental note of what no one mentions: how the city hospitals will fill up with what they call "social admissions," people who come into the emergency room pleading suicidal thoughts, knowing that the hospital is obligated to give them beds. Michael won't be among them—as far as I know he's never been overtly suicidal or conniving. He'll be on his own, doing his best to evade capture.

Stay warm, I catch myself mumbling, and there comes this icy chill fitted over my heart, precisely, like a cap of snow.

By half-past, I should be stepping out into the weather. I'm trying to start earlier to allow for a different route to work each time. I'm doing my damndest to keep my eyes peeled.

When people die they turn away and forever after, in my mind's eye, I see them with faces turned to the darkness or to the light but never again to me. That hasn't happened with Michael. That's why I think he's still alive.

Out on the street this morning it's every bit as cold as promised. My breath rises up to meet me in clumps, in dandelion puffs and tatters that tell me I'm thinking out loud again. But so what if I am? The man I'm about to pass is wrapped to his eyes in a woolen scarf; he won't be able to hear a thing.

So I let it rip. My little mantra, crazy, but it helps, but only for a second—

Do you feel the air move when I pass? When I think of you?

My eyes brim (but it's the cold that does it), the street blurs and glistens.

Michael?

No—but I'll find him. It's not impossible; he's got to be out there somewhere. All I ask is to know. Even if he's out on the road now, he'll come back to the city eventually (he always has), and it must be at least possible that, walking to work one day, I'll spot him up ahead, waiting for the light to change. I won't be surprised when he pivots suddenly, full face to me, and raises one hand, palm flat out, the signal unmistakable: *Stay. Come no closer*—

And I'll stand at a sort of salute, watching him fade, my enforced stillness as great an exertion as running.

No one could ever call it resting.

AUTHOR'S NOTE

I wish to thank Pamela Collins for pointing out the Lovell article containing the case history upon which my story is based.

Although I have turned to the texts and case material listed below for authentication, inspiration, or provocation while composing this book, the reader must remember that this is a work of fiction.

Anonymous. *The Cloud of Unknowing*. Edited by James Walsh, S.J. New York: Paulist Press, 1981.

Chadwick, P., and C. Lowe. "Measurement and Modification of Delusional Beliefs." *Journal of Consulting and Clinical Psychology* 58 (1990): 225–32, cited in Walkup.

Coetzee, J. M. "At the Gate." Chap. 8 in *Elizabeth Costello*. New York: Viking, 2003.

Crashaw, Richard. Versicle and responsory from "The Howres" in *The Office of the Holy Crosse*, 1648.

Lovell, Anne M. "The City Is My Mother: Narratives of Schizophrenia and Homelessness." *American Anthropologist* 99, no. 2 (June 1997): 355–68.

Sass, Louis A. *The Paradoxes of Delusion: Wittgenstein, Schreber, and the Schizophrenic Mind*. Ithaca, N.Y.: Cornell University Press, 1994.

Schreber, Daniel Paul. *Memoirs of My Nervous Illness*. Translated by Ida Macalpine and Richard A. Hunter. 1955. Reprint, New York: New York Review Books, 2000.

Walkup, James. "A Clinically Based Rule of Thumb for Classifying Delusions." *Schizophrenia Bulletin* 21, no. 2 (1995): 323–31.

White, E. B. "Here in New York." In *Essays of E. B. White*. New York: Harper & Row, 1977. "The eighteen inches were both the connection and the separation that New York provides for its inhabitants," p. 119.

Additionally, in moving through this narrative, the reader should be warned of rustlings behind the curtain, whispers, echoes, footprints—hauntings by one or another unnamed literary ghost.

A. G. Mojtabai is the author of eight novels, including *All That Road Going* (Northwestern, 2008). She has also published the short-story collection *Soon: Tales from Hospice* and the nonfiction study *Blessèd Assurance: At Home with the Bomb in Amarillo, Texas*.